Was He In Love?

Eric honestly didn't know, because he'd never been in love, except with a blue-eyed, raven-haired minx who'd sat next to him in the fourth grade, and that didn't count.

Besides, probing his emotions wasn't one of his usual practices. But unless he did a little psyche-digging, examining the available evidence as he would in relation to his police work, how else could he form an intelligent opinion?

After all these years of uncomplicated, uninvolved bliss, why had Eric Wolfe gone and fallen for a suspect?

BIG, BAD WOLFE SERIES: Four handsome, hardworking brothers who lay down the law—each one bigger and badder than the next!

Dear Reader,

Readers ask me what *I* think Silhouette Desire is. To me, Desire love stories are sexy, sassy, emotional and dynamic books about the power of love.

I demand variety, and strive to bring you six unique stories each month. These stories might be quite different, but each promises a wonderful love story with a happy ending.

This month, there's something I know you've all been waiting for: the next installment in Joan Hohl's *Big, Bad Wolfe* series, July's *Man of the Month, Wolfe Watching*. Here, undercover cop Eric Wolfe falls hard for a woman who is under suspicion.... Look for more *Big, Bad Wolfe* stories later in 1994.

As for the rest of July, well, things just keep getting hotter, starting with *Nevada Drifter,* a steamy ranch story from Jackie Merritt. And if you like your Desire books fun and sparkling, don't miss Peggy Moreland's delightful *The Baby Doctor*.

As all you "L.A. Law" fans know, there's nothing like a good courtroom drama (I *love* them myself!), so don't miss Doreen Owens Malek's powerful, gripping love story *Above the Law*. Of course, if you'd rather read about single moms trying to get single guys to love them—*and* their kids—don't miss Leslie Davis Guccione's *Major Distractions*.

To complete July we've found a tender, emotional story from a wonderful writer, Modean Moon. The book is titled *The Giving*, and it's a bit different for Silhouette Desire, so please let me know what you think about this very special love story.

So there you have it: drama, romance, humor and suspense, all rolled into six books in one fabulous line—Silhouette Desire. Don't miss any of them.

All the best,

Lucia Macro
Senior Editor

JOAN HOHL

WOLFE WATCHING

ISBN 0-373-05865-9

WOLFE WATCHING

This edition published by arrangement with Harlequin Enterprises B. V.

Printed in U.S.A.

Books by Joan Hohl

Silhouette Desire

A Much Needed Holiday #247
**Texas Gold* #294
**California Copper* #312
**Nevada Silver* #330
Lady Ice #354
One Tough Hombre #372
Falcon's Flight #390
The Gentleman Insists #475
Christmas Stranger #540
Handsome Devil #612
Convenient Husband #732
Lyon's Cub #762
+*Wolfe Waiting* #806
+*Wolfe Watching* #865

*Desire Trilogy
+Big, Bad Wolfe series

Silhouette Intimate Moments

Moments Harsh, Moments Gentle #35

Silhouette Special Edition

Thorne's Way #54
Forever Spring #444
Thorne's Wife #537

Silhouette Romance

A Taste for Rich Things #334
Someone Waiting #358
The Scent of Lilacs #376

Silhouette Books

Silhouette Summer Sizzlers 1988
"Grand Illusion"

Silhouette Christmas Stories 1993
"Holiday Homecoming"

JOAN HOHL

is the author of almost three dozen books. She has received numerous awards for her work, including the Romance Writers of America Golden Medallion. In addition to contemporary romance, this prolific author also writes historical and time-travel romances. Joan lives in eastern Pennsylvania with her husband and family.

One

She was a breath stopper.

Eric Wolfe inhaled and watched the young woman exit the house and stride along the flagged path to the sidewalk, hang a left, then head right toward where he was making a pretense of working on his bike in the driveway of the residence three properties down from her own.

The honey blonde wasn't very big; she was really quite petite, but every inch of her was packed with feminine dynamite.

Her delicate features fit perfectly in her heart-shaped face. Brown eyebrows gently arched over dark brown eyes fringed by incredibly long eyelashes, lending an overall appearance of wide-eyed innocence.

Right.

Eric's mouth slanted at a cynical angle.

Her name was Christina Marianna Kranas. Her friends called her Tina. She appeared to be something of a contradiction. She rarely, if ever, dated one-on-one, and yet she very obviously enjoyed her nights out and a good time. And she had lots of male, as well as female, friends.

Eric wasn't one of them. He was a neighbor, a relatively new and temporary neighbor. But Eric knew just about all there was to know about her.

Born and raised in Philadelphia, Christina Kranas was twenty-six years and four months old. She had married in haste at the advanced age of twenty-one. It hadn't worked. The man had a criminal record—he had been collared and booked numerous times—but he had never served time. There had never been enough hard evidence to prosecute with any hope of getting a conviction. Christina had claimed she didn't know about his scrapes with the law.

Eric was reserving judgment on her claim.

The marriage had quickly disintegrated, barely lasting eighteen months. The union had been childless. Christina had been granted a divorce almost four years ago.

Eric was less than impressed, since the man continued to pay periodic visits to her...and his best friend, who just happened to own and live in the house across the street, the house Eric had under observation.

Too convenient by far.

Her former husband was a good-looking guy named Glen Reber. Christina had assumed her maiden name upon receiving her divorce decree.

She had also assumed the responsibility for the mortgage on the small ranch-style house on the quiet street in the middle-income section located on the very edge of Philadelphia's city limits. She owned and operated a classy-looking florist shop in center city.

Christina stood exactly five-foot-two-and-three-quarter-inches tall. She maintained a weight of ninety-eight-and-one-half pounds—discounting normal monthly fluctuations. She wore a size 32B bra, size 5A shoes, and a size 3 petite dress, depending on the maker and quality of the garment. Her ring size was also a 5.

Eric knew all Christina's vital statistics because he had made it his business to know; committing to memory every factor gleaned about a possible suspect was part of his job.

He took his job very seriously; he always had, and even more so since the death of his father at the hands of a strung-out cocaine dealer during a drug bust three years ago.

At present, Christina was striding along in low-heeled size 5 shoes, making for the bus stop at the corner, because her car had been in a repair shop for three days to meet State inspection standards. And his presence in the driveway at this precise time of the morning was not a mere coincidence.

Eric ran an encompassing, if unobtrusive, glance over Christina's enticing form as she drew closer to him. Her outfit was both casual and smart looking. She had great taste. The observation was not a new one for him. He had reached the conclusion about her style at first sight of her, which had occurred nearly a week ago, on the very day he moved into the bachelor apartment above the garage attached to the three-bedroom house.

Eric had also concluded that watching Tina was the one pleasurable side benefit of the unpleasant business associated with being an undercover police officer.

Eric was good at his chosen profession; he knew he was, in all probability, good at it because he liked being a cop. It ran in the family. Generations of Wolfe men had served the law, in one form or another. The third of four sons, all in law enforcement, Eric was the only one who had followed his father into the force in Philadelphia.

He had volunteered for undercover work in the narcotics division after his father was gunned down in the line of duty.

Only, in this instance, Eric was working under his own auspices; he was officially on vacation. He had requested leave time after receiving a tip from one of his informants, a tip that had fired his anger.

The informant had told Eric that the latest word on the street was that there were dealers—ostensibly an ordinary middle-class couple—doing business out of their home in this quiet community minutes away from center city.

While important, that information alone had not been the catalyst that motivated Eric. It was the informant's claim that the couple had been the suppliers to the man who had shot Eric's father that had been the factor in determining his actions.

Eric wanted vengeance—and he wasn't inclined toward having his methods questioned by the department. Fully aware that he could be summarily dismissed from the force if he screwed up, he had decided to take vacation leave in order to play a hunch.

Since the hunch and the subsequent idea of taking up residence in the neighborhood were his, to all intents and purposes he was on his own. Eric rather liked the idea.

Eric had been maintaining surveillance on Christina for a week now. He had been open in his movements, visible as he tinkered with his bike in the driveway, pleasant in response to greetings offered by passing residents, but he had yet to exchange a word with her.

Today was the day.

Pulling a rag from his back jeans pocket, Eric slowly straightened to his full six-foot-four-inch height. He flashed his most charming smile as he casually wiped his hands on the grimy cloth.

"'Morning," he said as she drew even with him.

Christina started, as if rudely jolted from introspection by the sound of his voice. Her smooth stride faltered.

Eric controlled the smile itching to become a grin.

"Ah...good morning..." she returned, her lips forming a tentative smile, while her eyebrows crept together in a frown.

"Beautiful day," Eric observed, keeping her from rushing on. "Unusually warm for November."

"Yes...er, it is..." she agreed, taking a step forward to resume her brisk pace.

"Want a lift?" His offer brought her up short once more. "I think I've finally solved the problem here." He waved a hand at the bike. "I'm going into town."

Christina shifted a leery look from her soft gray wool slacks and matching hip-length jacket to the Harley. "Ah...I don't think so, thank you."

"It's clean," he assured her, flicking the rag at a nonexistent speck of dust on the gleaming silver-and-black machine. "And I have an extra helmet."

"No, really, I..."

"There goes your bus." Eric indicated the corner intersection with a nod of his head and smiled ruefully. "I'm sorry. I'm afraid I made you miss it." He raised his eyebrows. "How long before the next bus?"

She sighed. "Half hour."

"My offer of a lift is still open," he said, in a tone designed to convey his eagerness to be of help.

Christina stood, silent and uncertain, for several seconds, and then she sighed again. "Okay, thank you."

Eric turned away to head for the garage—and to hide a smile of satisfaction. "I'll get the helmet... back in a sec."

A motorcycle. Suppressing yet another sigh, Christina stood staring at the shiny bike. A big, dangerous motorcyle, driven by a man she didn't know from Adam.

Not too bright, Tina, she told herself, even if the man did happen to look like a walking, talking twentieth-century version of a classic Greek god.

Only this particular Greek god had the formidable appearance of a modern-day Teutonic warrior.

Christina felt a delicate tingle skip up her spine. He was one attractive representative of the male species. Crystal blue eyes gazed out at the world from beneath a shock of wavy golden brown hair. His facial bone structure was chiseled, defined by high cheekbones, a straight, aristocratic nose, a strong, squared jawline and a mouth that held a promise of inflicting infinite pleasure... or pain.

The speculation intensified the tingle in Tina's now-stiffened spine. What had she let herself in for here? she wondered anxiously. She didn't even know this man's name, for pete's sake! And he literally towered over her.

Tina judged him to be at least six-three, possibly six-four, and without a visible ounce of excess flesh on that lean, flatly muscled frame.

And she had agreed to ride away with him on that monstrous machine. Was she nuts, or what? she asked herself, glancing around, as if for an avenue of escape. If she had any sense left at all, Tina thought, she'd take off at once and, if necessary, run all the way into center city.

"Name's Eric, by the way."

Tina's body jerked with mild shock at the sudden sound of his voice. But she managed to swallow the yelp of surprise that sprang to her throat at the sight of him standing beside the bike, his face concealed by a black-visored helmet. She drew a measure of reassurance from the fact that he didn't look anything like her preconceived notion of a leathered, chained, tattooed biker. But, on the other hand, he looked too appealing with his lean body clad in tight jeans, chest-caressing pullover sweater and expensive, if rather beat-up, running shoes.

"Eric... Wolfe."

What else? Tina squashed the nerve-jangling observation, along with her senses-stirring response to the low, attractive sound of his voice.

"I moved in a week ago."

"Ah...how do you do?" Great response, Tina, she chided herself, reluctantly extending her right hand. His hand, long, broad, slim fingered and strong, shot out to enclose hers, drawing the tingle from her spine to her fingertips—and every inch in between. "I'm Christina Kranas," she said, sliding her palm away from the too-warm, strangely intimate touch of his. "I live three houses down."

"I know."

Coming from behind that black visor, his simple reply had an ominous overtone that further intensified the tingle now jabbing throughout the entire length of Tina's body. "Really?" she said, infusing coolness into her usually low, somewhat throaty voice.

"Sure." His voice carried an unmistakable smile. "Couldn't help but notice you... the times I've been out here, working on the bike, you know?"

"Oh." The stiffness eased a little inside Tina; his explanation did have a reasonable ring. "Ah, yes, I see." But why hadn't she noticed him? she mused, skimming a quick glance over his person. He was pretty hard to miss, and—

"Chris for short?"

His question derailed the train of her thoughts. "Chris?" She frowned, then shook her head when his meaning registered. "No. Tina."

"Umm. Makes sense." Now his voice contained a definite shade of muffled laughter. "Well, then, Tina..." He made a sweeping gesture with his arm. "Ready to go?"

No. Tina clamped her lips against the sharp refusal; she *had* agreed to the lift. "Yes...I suppose so." Even she could hear the lack of conviction in her voice.

"It's perfectly safe," he said reassuringly, holding the helmet out to her with one hand while lifting a windbreaker from the seat of the bike with the other.

"I...um, it looks so powerful," she said, her stomach clenching as she watched the play of shoulder and chest muscles as he shrugged into the windbreaker.

"It is." Raising a hand, he flipped up the visor to grin at her, and dazzle her with his white teeth. "But I can handle the beast."

Despite her trepidation, Tina felt a smile tug at her lips; this man was not without charm. "Well...okay." Drawing a breath, she took the helmet and eased it over her head, careful not to dislodge the neat pleat she had folded her long hair into at the back. Fully expecting to have her vision curtailed by the dark visor, she was surprised by the range of visibility it afforded her. "How do I...er...mount?" she asked, eyeing the bike with suspicion from behind the dark cover.

"Like this." Still grinning, Eric swung his right leg up and over the bike, then stood straddling it. "Come on," he urged. "You're wearing pants."

Oh, what the hell. So thinking, Tina marched to the side of the bike and swung her own leg up and over. Although she completed the exercise, her effort did not bear comparison to his for smooth adroitness. When she was in position, he flipped down his visor and lowered his long torso onto the seat.

"Okay, settle in behind me," Eric directed, effortlessly holding the machine upright and steady. "Then grab on to my waist, my belt...or whatever, and hang on."

Tina bristled at the slight accent he had placed on the "whatever," but she followed his instructions, opting for his belt.

"By the way, where do you want to go?"

"Oh, you can drop me off anywhere close to Wannamaker's," she answered, distracted by his question.

Eric flipped a switch; the beast growled to life and an instant later roared out of the driveway and turned left onto the street, sounding beautifully tuned and in perfect running condition.

Exclaiming at the sudden burst of motion in a startled shriek, which went unheard over the roar of the bike, Tina tightened her grasp on his belt and hung on for dear life, shutting her eyes tight as Eric whipped in and out around the snaking lines of rush-hour traffic.

Every muscle in Tina's body was quivering by the time Eric glided the bike to a smooth stop along the curb opposite one of the wide showroom windows of Wannamaker's department store.

"Thank... thank you," Tina said, breathless and still quivering as she scrambled off the machine he thoughtfully tilted toward the pavement for her. Feet once more firmly on the ground, she removed the helmet and handed it to him.

Eric accepted the headgear with a shrug. "Anytime." He paused, then quickly qualified, "That is, anytime I'm off from work, like today."

Tina raised her brows. "Friday is your day off?"

"No." He shook his head. "Ah, I'm on vacation leave." He arched a toast-colored eyebrow. "You work nearby?"

"Yes. I own a flower shop on Chestnut Street." Tina gave him a smile of pure envy. "I wish I could take a vacation but with the holidays coming up, I can't afford the time." She sighed. Then, reminded of work, she glanced at her watch. "I have to go. Thanks again."

"Sure." Eric sketched a wave, the bike growled, and then he roared away from the curb, leaving her standing there, inhaling exhaust fumes and staring after him.

Shaking her head, Tina took a tentative step, testing the steadiness of her legs. She was still feeling a little quivery and mildly shocked from the mad dash into town. And yet, at the same time, she felt wildly exhilarated, and more vibrantly alive than she had in ages.

All of which had absolutely nothing to do with the residue of warmth simmering in her thighs from being pressed tightly against Eric Wolfe's narrow buttocks, Tina bracingly assured herself as she joined the forward thrust of the pedestrian traffic hurrying along the sidewalk.

* * *

He could still feel the pressure of her legs clamped to his butt.

Weaving in and out of the crowded city traffic, Eric shifted in the saddle and grinned behind the visor. Felt good, too, he decided, savoring the physical sensation.

Due to the increasing demands of his work, very real and considerable current health concerns and a lack of time for much of a social life, it had been a while, a good long while, since Eric had enjoyed the pleasure derived from a woman's legs wrapped around him—for any reason.

So, in light of his self-imposed celibacy, Eric told himself, the reactions he was now experiencing were perfectly normal, if a bit intense. And they certainly were intense, with fiery strands of sensation coiling around the sides of his hips and converging in a most vulnerable section of his body.

Eric attempted to moisten his parched lips with a quick glide of his tongue; it didn't help much. His tongue was every bit as dry as his lips.

Wild.

Eric utilized an enforced wait for a traffic light to ponder these not-at-all-normal physical responses. All this heat from the feel of Tina's wool-covered legs clasped to his jeans-clad hips? he marveled, revving the motor impatiently. What in hell would it do to him, how would it feel, to be cradled by her silky thighs, naked flesh pressed to naked flesh?

It would feel good . . . maybe too damn good.

Keep your mind on the business at hand, Wolfe, Eric advised himself, shifting once more in the bike's saddle to ease a gathering tightness in his body, and zooming through the intersection when the light blinked to green.

Business.

Hell.

Gripping the handlebars, Eric swooped around the slow-moving car of ancient vintage putt-putting in front of him. The business at hand concerned the illegal possession and sale of narcotics. A nasty business, and very likely conducted to the tune of millions of dollars.

And he was fairly certain that business was being conducted in that ordinary-looking middle-income house across the street and down a few properties from the garage apartment he had so recently moved into.

What Eric wasn't at all certain of was the possible involvement—or lack thereof—of one Christina Marianna Kranas in that nasty business.

The question mark stabbed at Eric's mind as persistently as the memory of her encasing legs stabbed at his body.

"Ouch!"

"You okay, Tina?" Susan Grant poked her head around the doorway into the workroom.

"Yeah." Tina's self-disgust was evident, even with the tip of her finger stuck in her mouth. "I pricked my finger on a corsage pin," she explained to her frowning assistant.

"You've been kind of not quite with it all morning," Susan said, stepping through the doorway separating the workroom from the showroom. "Something bothering you?"

Not something, someone.

Keeping the thought where it belonged, inside her rattled mind, Tina shook her head. "No, I guess I'm just a little distracted today."

Susan's frown dissolved into a teasing smile. "Thinking about tonight...and Ted Saunders?"

"Well...perhaps." Tina forced a light-sounding laugh and turned back to the worktable. Her answer had verged on an outright lie. No "perhaps" about it...she hadn't given a single thought to the coming evening or her date with Ted. In fact, until Susan mentioned it, Tina had completely forgotten she had made a date for that evening. Why had she made a date with Ted for this evening?

Tina frowned. Oh, yeah, her car was in the shop. For that matter, she didn't really consider it a real date...even though Ted had been after her to go out with him for some weeks now. She had consistently put him off.

She would have put him off again when he called late yesterday afternoon, but Ted hadn't actually asked her for a date. Ted had asked her if she planned to join their group of mutual friends at their usual Friday-evening get-together at the tavern. Tina had told him she was. Knowing her car was in the shop for repairs, Ted had then offered to stop by her place and give her a lift to the tavern. Fully aware that he had his own agenda, that of convincing her to regard him in the role of prospective suitor, Tina had nevertheless accepted his offer with gratitude.

End of date business; she still had no intention of expanding their friendship into a more intimate relationship. She wasn't interested in any kind of male-female relationship other than friendship. She'd been that route; it had a lot of potholes and detours.

No, thoughts of the coming evening were not the cause of her state of mind, Tina acknowledged, jabbing the long, pearl-tipped pin through a stem on the elegant corsage—this time correctly. The root cause of her distraction stood six foot four, and possessed a lean, mean sexiness that wouldn't quit.

Wolfe.

Tina sighed.

What else?

Eric was bored. Bored and itchy. There wasn't a damn thing happening in the house across the street.

Deserting his position behind the lacy curtain at the solitary window in the minuscule living room of the bachelor flat, Eric prowled to the even tinier kitchen and pulled open the door of the compact apartment-size refrigerator.

"And when he got there, the fridge was bare," he paraphrased in a disgusted mutter.

Heaving a sigh, Eric inventoried the contents of the small unit. A quarter of a loaf of bread, a week past the sell-by date on the wrapper; one slice of lunch meat, curl dried around the edges because he hadn't rewrapped it properly; a small jar containing two olives, sans pimentos; a carton of milk; and a package of butterscotch Tastykakes.

Hardly the ingredients of a well-balanced dinner, he allowed, sighing once more as he shut the door. He really should have stopped at the supermarket on his way back from the city this morning . . . but then, Eric conceded, he really hadn't been concerned with his stomach this morning. His concern had centered on a lower portion of his anatomy.

Tooling a powerful bike through a city the size of Philly required concentration . . . plus the ability to sit comfortably in the saddle. And, with Tina's thighs pressed to his rump, Eric had lacked both requirements.

Would she be going to the tavern tonight?

The question had skipped in and out of his mind all through that boring day. From the detailed information he had received on her, compliments of his older brother, Cameron, an FBI agent, Eric knew that Tina generally met her friends at a neighborhood tavern on Fridays, for an evening of fun and frivolity.

Eric likewise knew that the tavern served up a decent charbroiled steak with side orders of tossed salad and Texas fries. He had heard, as well, that the pizza was first-rate. He loved charbroiled steak and Texas fries. Good pizza, too, come to that.

Should he?

His stomach grumbled.

Eric's smile was slow and feral.

Why the hell not?

Two

He stood out in the human crush like a fiery beacon on a fog-shrouded beach. The indirect amber lighting sparked bronze glints off his gold-streaked mane of tawny hair.

Tina spotted Eric Wolfe the instant she crossed the threshold into the dimly lit taproom. A frisson of shocked surprise rippled the length of her small frame; her step faltered; her thighs quivered with remembered warmth.

Appearing casual, as though her hesitation were deliberate, she studied him while making a show of glancing around the spacious room.

Eric stood propped against one end of the horseshoe-curved bar, his back to the wall. He was dressed casually, quite the same as that morning, but in newer tight jeans and a different, brown-and-white patterned sweater. His right hand was wrapped around a long-necked bottle of beer, which he intermittently sipped as he lazily surveyed the laughing, chattering patrons crowded into the noisy, smoky tavern.

"Do you see them?"

Tina's body reacted with a slight jolt to the intrusive sound of Ted's voice too close behind her. Them? She frowned. Oh, *them!* Reminded of her friends, Tina dragged her riveted gaze from the alluring form at the end of the bar and transferred it to the far corner of the room, where she and her friends usually congregated at two tables shoved together.

They were there, in force, all eight of them. Two of the women and one of the men had arms raised, hands waving, to catch her attention.

"Yes," she finally answered. "There in the back, at the same old stand."

"Here, let me go ahead," he said, moving in front of her. "I'll clear the way."

Following in Ted's footsteps, weaving in and out and around tables and the press of bodies standing by, reminded Tina of the ride that morning, and the man in command of the bike. She slid a sidelong glance at the bar, blinked when she saw the empty spot at the end of it, then crashed into a beefy man who had just shoved his chair away from a table and was half in, half out of his seat.

Yelping, the man stumbled backward. His shoulder collided with Tina's chest, knocking the breath from her body and sending her reeling. Oblivious to the mishap behind him, Ted plowed on toward the corner and their friends. Backpedaling, Tina careered off another patron and emitted a muffled shriek as she felt herself begin to go down.

A hard arm snaked around her waist, breaking her fall, steadying her, shooting fingers of heat from her midsection to her thighs. She knew who her rescuer was an instant before his low voice caressed her ears.

"Don't panic, thistle toes." His voice was low; his arm was strong, firm. "You're all right."

Tina didn't know if she felt insulted or amused by Eric's drawled remark; she did know she felt suddenly overwarm within the circle of his arm—overwarm, yet strangely protected and completely safe.

"Thank...you," she said, between restorative gulps of breath. "A person could get trampled in this herd."

Eric's smile stole her renewed breath. The laughter gleaming in his crystal blue eyes played hell with her still-wobbly equilibrium. A muscle in his arm flexed, sending rivulets of sensation dancing up her spine.

"You're welcome." Keeping his arm firmly in place around her waist, he turned his head to make a swift perusal of the room. When his glance came back to her, he arched his eyebrows promptingly. "Where were you heading?"

"Over there," Tina answered, indicating the front corner with a vague hand motion.

"What happened to your escort?" Eric's voice conveyed censure for the man's dereliction of duty in caring for her. "Did he desert you in this zoo?"

"He was clearing the way for me." Tina's smile was both faint and wry. Looking at the table, she saw that most of her friends were now on their feet, their conversation animated as they stared back at her. Ted stood next to the table, his expression a study in confusion and consternation.

"Looks to me like your native friends are getting restless," Eric observed.

"Yes...er, I'd better join them." Tina took a step, fully expecting him to remove his arm; it not only remained in place, it tightened, like a steel coil anchoring her to his side. He began to move, drawing her with him.

"This time, *I'll* run interference."

Turned out there was no interference to run; Eric's intimidating size, coupled with his air of self-confidence and determination, had the patrons clogging the spaces between the tables in their haste to get out of his way.

"Tina, what happened?" Ted demanded, eying Eric warily when they reached the table.

"It was nothing," she replied, trying to make light of the embarrassing incident.

"She could have been injured."

Tina shivered at the hard condemnation in Eric's tone, and saw Ted visibly flinch in reaction to the piercing stare from the taller man's laser-bright eyes.

"But I wasn't," she quickly inserted. "So let's forget it." Forcing a carefree-sounding laugh, she swept her friends with an encompassing look and rushed on, changing the subject. "I don't know about anyone else, but I'm starving."

"Relief's on the way." The assurance came from one of the men. "The pizza's been ordered and should be coming any minute now."

"Good." Smile in place, Tina turned back to Eric. "Thank you again. I..." she began, intending to gently but decisively dismiss him.

"We ordered plenty," a female voice piped in. "Would you care to join us, Mr.—?"

"Eric Wolfe," he supplied, extending a smile and his right hand to the man closest to him.

"Bill Devine." Bill grasped Eric's hand and jerked his head to indicate the woman next to him, the one who had initiated the introductions. "This is Nancy Wagner."

Nancy...supposedly her best friend! Tina fumed in silent frustration as the round-robin continued.

"Wayne Fritz."

"Georgine Cutler."

"Mike Konopelski."

"Vincent Forlini."

"Helen Elliot."

"Louise Parsons."

"Ted Saunders."

Eric's smile vanished as the circle was completed with Ted. His voice took on a hint of disdain; his handshake was insultingly brief. "Saunders."

A strained silence descended on the group around the table. A red tide rose from Ted's neck to his cheeks. Tina felt a stab of compassion at his obvious abashment, and a sense of astonishment at Eric's powerful effect on her friends. Eric had merely repeated Ted's name, and yet his tone, the look of him, had held the force of a hard body blow.

Tina's sense of compassion, and her underlying unease, lasted a moment, then dissolved into impatience and annoyance. With his attitude, by his very presence, Eric had thrown a pall over the congenial atmosphere, stifling the fun of the group's weekly get-together. Growing angry, determined to send him on his way, she opened her mouth to issue polite but pointed marching orders to him. The first word never cleared her lips.

"Heads up, folks!" The warning came from the waiter, who was bearing down on their combined tables, a large tray balanced on the fingertips of both upraised hands. "Pizza!"

The aroma wafting from the steam rising from the pies brought a wash of water into Tina's mouth. Her stomach rumbled, reminding her that she had skipped lunch. Tilting her head to look directly at Eric, she managed a parody of a smile, and attempted once more to send him packing.

"Ah...thanks again, I..." And once again she found herself unable to accomplish her goal.

"What do you say, Eric?" Mike—the rat—called from the far end of the table. "There's plenty of room, and pizza. Wanna join us?"

Apparently the moment of embarrassed silence was over.... Of course, Tina knew too well that her friends were never silenced for very long. They were too exuberant, bursting with youth and the joy of life. Staring into Eric's alert, watchful eyes, she narrowed her own in a bid to convey her reluctance to have him invade their clannish circle. Her empty stomach lurched at the smile that began in the depths of his eyes an instant before it was reflected in his lazy smile.

"Sure. Why not?" Eric shrugged, setting the muscles in his shoulders and chest into an impressive rippling motion beneath his sweater. "Thanks."

Ted moved forward to hold a chair for Tina.

Eric moved faster. With a casual-looking, smooth turn of his body, he blocked Ted's movement. Pulling one chair aside, he kept a firm hold on it while sliding another one out for Tina. The moment she was seated, he dropped into the one he was holding and drew it into the table next to hers. Ted was relegated to the only remaining chair...between Mike and Helen, at the far end of the other table.

"Hope you like your pizza loaded, Eric," Bill said, grinning. "We ordered the works on both."

"I like it any way I can get it," Eric drawled, slanting a hooded, sultry look at Tina that implied something other and much more intimate than pizza. "But I like it best spicy and sizzling hot."

Denying the flare of response that leapt to life deep inside her, Tina glared a warning at him before turning away.

"So what are we waiting for?" Helen wailed from the end of the table. "Serve it up!"

In between bursts of conversation and laughter, the pies were parceled out and demolished. When it became clear that appetites were still unsatisfied, more pizza and fresh drinks were ordered. It was a normal Friday night.

Not quite normal, Tina mused, squirming in the allotted space afforded her between Eric on one side and Vincent on the other. On a normal Friday night, she could relax away the tensions of the workday, not have the tension increased by the sensations instilled by a hard thigh pressing against her leg, a muscled shoulder nudging her arm, a pair of crystalline blue eyes probing into her thoughts.

Tina's appetite for pizza deserted her, replaced by a different, sharper hunger below her stomach. Forcing herself to chew and swallow the food she no longer desired, and refusing to acknowledge the sensual craving, Tina managed to consume two slices of the pie without choking.

Next to her, Wolfe wolfed down half a dozen slices between pulls on another beer. Nothing wrong with his appetite, she thought, sliding a wry look at him.

Correctly interpreting her expression, Eric grinned, and once again set his shoulder and chest muscles into action with a careless shrug.

Tina shot an arched look back at him.

"I was hungry," he said, pressing his hard thigh more firmly against hers. "Still am," he went on, in a lower, breathy murmur. "But not for pizza."

Shock—or something—zigzagged through Tina. She went cold, stiff as a board, outside—and hot, soft as warmed satin, inside. The sensation of craving deep within her contracted into a tight mass of need, expanding the sense of shock to the farthest reaches of her body and mind.

What was happening to her? she marveled in confused silence. What kind of sensual power did Eric Wolfe possess to so effortlessly affect her in this manner? She hadn't experienced such a compelling carnal compulsion since—

Tina's mental process stalled, then raced forward, blurting the truth into her disbelieving consciousness. Never before in her life had she experienced such a depth of carnal compulsion. Not even with her husband. Not on his most potent night, or day, had Glen ever managed to arouse her in body or mind to the degree that Eric Wolfe had accomplished with smoldering glances, murmured innuendos and the relatively minor pressure of his thigh and shoulder against her own.

It was weird. It was scary. It was not to be tolerated, Tina decided, edging closer to Vincent. She didn't appreciate this hot-and-cold, hard-and-soft reaction to what, in fact, were the blandest of advances.

"Another drink?"

Tina's thoughts fractured. Blinking, she turned to face Eric, certain her expression was every bit as blank as her mind. "Ah...what?"

"Would you like another seltzer?" He inclined his head, indicating the tall glass in front of her, empty except for a wedge of lime and three half-melted ice cubes.

Feeling dull witted, Tina stared at the glass in bemusement, wondering when she had drunk the fizzy water...and why her throat still felt so dry.

"The waiter's waiting." Eric's droll drawl snagged her attention. "Would you like another?"

"No. Thank you." Tina shook her head. She felt suddenly tired, drained by the interior havoc created by this too-attractive, too-sexy, too-*close* man. "It's been a long day." Beginning with a short, wild ride, she added to herself. "I'd like to go home."

"I'll take you."

On that silver-and-black monster? Tina stifled the question, and shook her head again. "No, you won't," she said with tight asperity. "I came with Ted, I'll go home with him."

"Yes, but when?" Eric sent a pointed glance at Ted, then back to her.

Leaning forward, she gazed down the length of the tables to where Ted was engaged in a heated political discussion with Helen, Mike and Louise. At that moment, the waiter set a full mug of beer in front of him. Obviously Ted hadn't given a thought to leaving yet; it was still early, after all.

"Whenever." Tina lifted her shoulders in what she hoped conveyed an attitude of indifference she was far from feeling. "I think I will have another seltzer, after all."

Cool. Christina Kranas was one cool cookie.

Interesting, Eric mused, how the so-very-cool cookie called Tina could activate his personal heat button. Concealing a sardonic smile, he turned away and raised a hand to attract the waiter's attention.

After placing her drink order—seltzer? Eric grimaced—he shifted around to her again, only to find that Tina had turned her back to him to join in on a conversation in progress between Vincent and Bill.

Lazing in the chair, Eric monitored the discussion on the pros and cons of the current professional football season, and various teams, primarily the Philadelphia Eagles, while at the same time doing some professional work of his own, that of evaluating the members of Tina's close-knit group.

They appeared ordinary enough—all-American, clean-cut, ages running from the mid- to late twenties, upper-middle to middle class, well educated, motivated, career minded. Everyday, normal, innocent.

Maybe.

Then again, maybe not. Eric hadn't remained alive by relying on guesswork. He wasn't about to begin now. Although he regretted having to do so, he would have to go back to the well of information at the fingertips of one special agent for the FBI, his brother, Cameron Wolfe—referred to by his fellow agents as the Lone Wolfe.

Eric was prepared to endure the ribbing Cameron would most assuredly give him about a member of the force having to once again come begging for assistance from a federal agent. His brother's teasing was nothing new, and it was a price Eric was more than willing to pay.

Raising his arm, Eric took a small swig from the long-necked bottle, swishing the beer around inside his mouth before letting the brew trickle down his throat. The bottle was his second for the night... his second and his last.

Eric knew better than to overindulge at any time. A soused undercover cop had even less value than a soused anyone else, and was potentially a lot more dangerous... to himself, to the force and to bystanders, innocent or otherwise.

"Aren't you about ready for another beer, Eric?" Bill asked, almost as if he had tapped into the other man's thought process. "You've been nursing that one since right after you sat down. Hell, the rest of us are on our fourth."

No kidding? Eric mentally responded, lips curling into a rueful smile. "Two's my limit," he said truthfully. "I can't tolerate more than that, it goes to my head," he explained, lying without compunction.

"Bummer." The unsolicited opinion came from Vincent. "I can knock 'em back all night without getting woozy."

"Yeah, you just can't drive," Bill retorted.

Vincent shrugged. "I don't have to." He favored Tina with a sweet smile. "We have a nondrinker in the group."

Eric had known from the investigative report his brother had provided for him that Tina rarely indulged in any kind of alcoholic drinks, the exception being the occasional celebratory half glass of champagne at holidays, weddings and such. He hadn't known that she was the designated driver for the less prudent members of her circle of friends. He again arched a brow at her.

"You're the official D.C., huh?"

Tina frowned. "D.C.?"

"Drunk chauffeur," he explained, grinning to ease the sting from the expression.

"Hey, I resent that," Vincent protested, loud enough to be heard over Bill's eruption of laughter.

"Sorry, no offense meant." Though Eric offered the apology to Vincent, he kept his gaze steady on Tina.

"I don't mind." She was quick to the defense. "It doesn't happen too often . . . and they are my friends. And I prefer having them alive."

"Thatta girl, Tina," Vincent crowed, raising his frothy mug in salute to her, while leveling a smug look at Eric. "She doesn't want to see this handsome face and body all torn and mangled in a wreck of metal."

"Oh, brother." Bill rolled his eyes.

"No, it's true," Tina said, her smile soft, maternal. "I don't want to ever see any of my friends or anybody else for that matter torn and mangled."

Eric felt an odd little catch at the base of his throat at the softness of her smile, the caring sound of her voice. It was not the sound or look one would expect from a woman involved, even peripherally, with the pushing of narcotics.

Chill out, Wolfe, he advised himself, taking a sip of the now-warm beer to dislodge the catch. More than most, he knew how deceptive appearances could be.

Take this group, for example, he mused, shifting his eyes from Tina's tender expression to sweep the occupants of the two tables with a swift but encompassing glance.

They all appeared to be perfectly normal, average, law-abiding citizens. But were they? Ah, there's the question, Eric thought, appearing quite normal and average himself as he laughed at a quip from Bill. He was in a particularly good position to know that appearances quite often did not reflect reality.

From the bits and pieces he had picked up from the conversations around the table during the demolition of the pizza—which had actually exceeded its reputation—Eric had gleaned the information that the careers of the individuals were diverse, ranging from carpenter to corporate middle manager and several different job descriptions in between, including Tina's ownership of the florist shop. All quite normal, with such a varied assortment of individuals.

Perhaps. Keeping his expression free of his speculative thoughts, Eric skimmed the faces around him. But on the other hand, he reasoned, for all he and the world knew, this varied assortment of individuals with diverse career pursuits might well be in the business of supplementing their incomes with the profits garnered by dealing in illegal substances.

Of course, the world would continue to revolve in its ignorance. Eric fully intended to glean the necessary information, first thing in the morning, or as soon as Cameron could gather it for him.

The search might prove fruitless. Eric hoped it would; he was enjoying their company. Nevertheless, the investigation and follow-up would be done, whether the results were good, bad or merely indifferent.

Meanwhile, there was a question about Tina. A very big, very unsavory question.

Was she mixed up in a narcotics mess?

Her attractive peal of laughter drew Eric's attention—and his hooded eyes—to her profile. She was looking at Nancy at the end of the second table, laughing appreciatively at whatever the other woman had said. Once again he felt that odd catch in his throat.

Why did she have to be so damned appealing? Eric asked himself, studying her with an appearance of lazy disinterest. The problem was, there wasn't a thing lazy or disinterested about his perusal of her.

Merely looking at Tina reactivated the memory of her slender thighs banding his hips and posterior, driving a wedge of heat to the apex of his thighs.

Damn. He was hard. Eric drew a long, slow breath and shifted unobtrusively in the chair, easing his leg to the side, away from the too-enticing touch of hers.

What was it about this particular woman? he wondered, sketching his gaze over Tina, from the top of her shimmering blond hair to the slender ankles beneath the hem of her wool slacks, lingering on the gentle curves in between.

She was attractive.... Okay, she was more than attractive, he conceded. Her petite frame held infinite allure. Her face, though not classically beautiful, was delicately featured, lovely, with that mass of honey blond hair contrasted with dark brown eyes and brows and an abundance of long lashes above a small, straight nose and a delectable pair of lips made for crushing by a man's passion-hardened mouth.

Eric swallowed a groan and shifted again. What in hell was he doing to himself? Now he was not only hard, he was hot and uncomfortable, and he had completely lost the thread of the ongoing conversation.

Maybe it was time to cut out of here, he thought. Get some fresh air. Get some rest. *Get a grip.*

Lifting a hand to his mouth, Eric covered a manufactured yawn. "Well, I don't know about the rest of you folks," he announced, pushing his chair back away from the table, distancing himself from Tina. "But I'm ready for bed."

"Yeah, me too," Bill said, stifling a genuine yawn. "I've got to work tomorrow."

Three of the others agreed that it was time to leave, since they also had to work. The remaining members of the group protested. Tina stayed silent, but stared at Ted in mute supplication.

"But it's not that late," Helen pointed out.

"Only a little after twelve," Mike said, glancing at his watch.

"We can stay for a while," Ted insisted, seemingly unconscious of the appeal in Tina's eyes. "You're not ready, are you, Tina?"

"If you wouldn't mind, Ted." Though she smiled, she also sighed. "I'm tired, and I have a lot of orders to get out early tomorrow morning."

Ted frowned.

Figuring it was worth one more shot, Eric spoke up. "I can take Tina along with me, Ted, if you want to stay. I live right up the street from her."

"You do?"

Though Ted asked the question, all the others looked at Eric in surprise.

"Yes." Eric smiled. "I moved into the neighborhood a couple of days ago."

"Well..." Ted began uncertainly.

"No." Tina's smile was pleasant, but her tone was adamant. "We can stay for a little while, Ted."

Good-nights were exchanged, and Eric turned to leave. As he did, he caught the glow of triumph gleaming in the brown depths of Tina's eyes.

Think you've won, do you? A grin twitched Eric's lips as he strode for the exit. Tina, my sweet, all you've won is a minor skirmish, he told her in silent amusement.

We'll see who wins the war.

Three

The city transit bus ran over a pothole. The resulting bump shuddered through the vehicle and the few remaining passengers still on board near the end of the line.

The jarring sensation rippled up Tina's spine to the back of her neck, aggravating the throbbing pain in her temples. The pain had been little more than an annoying ache when she awakened that morning. Not enough sleep, she had thought, dragging her tired body from the bed to the bathroom.

A stinging shower had not revived her lethargic body or relieved the ache in her head. Telling herself that she should have insisted Ted bring her home at a reasonable hour didn't help much, either. Tina hadn't insisted; Ted and the others who had remained in the tavern had lingered on long after the rest of their friends had called it a night, talking and drinking, until the bartender had shouted his nightly last-call-for-drinks warning. And even then she had not been able to go directly home, as she had assumed the responsibility of driving Ted and the others to their respective homes.

Then, with the prolonged goodbyes at each successive house or apartment, it had been very late when she finally crawled into bed.

When she left her house that morning, Ted's car was parked in her driveway. Although Ted had urged her to use it to get to work, Tina had flatly refused, unwilling to take on the added responsibility of driving his fairly new car in the morning and evening rush hours.

And so, in consequence, simply getting herself out of bed and together and to the corner bus stop was like pushing a rope uphill . . . with her nose.

The thought had sprung to mind, more than once, that perhaps she should have accepted the offer of a lift home last night from her new neighbor. Tina had pushed the thought aside every time it insinuated itself into her consciousness—for what she felt were excellent reasons.

Eric Wolfe was too good to look at, too charming, too...too masculine. The merest consideration of the tall, gorgeous, tawny-haired hunk sent Tina's pulses into overdrive and her breathing processes into decline, and set her thighs to tingling in remembrance of being pressed to his firm, jean-clad tush.

And it simply was not like her to react in such a manner to a man—any man. Her blatantly sensual response confused Tina; hadn't her former husband cruelly accused her of being cold, lacking normal sensuality?

Upon long consideration of her unresponsiveness to Glen's lovemaking, and the attempted advances made by other men since her divorce, hadn't she been forced to concede to the validity of his claim?

Sadly, Tina had to admit that in all honesty, the answer to her own questions had to be yes.

But then, if Glen's accusations, and her reluctant agreement with them were accurate, why did her mind persist in envisioning a man she hardly knew? Tina wondered, her headache made worse by the questions hammering at her.

Then, as if mentally dodging the tormenting images of one unmentionable man wasn't enough, business in the shop had been brisk, demanding her scattered attention. Consequently, her headache had steadily increased throughout the seemingly endless day. And now, past six-thirty in the evening, all she wanted to do was swallow two aspirins, lie down and hopefully escape from her unwelcome contemplation of one particular man, while sleeping off the pounding pain in her head. But first she had to get home.

The bus creaked and groaned to a stop. Tina exhaled a sigh of relief; the next stop was hers. Then again . . . maybe some exercise in the crisp autumn air would be as beneficial as sleep and painkillers.

"Please wait!" she called to the driver as she jumped from her seat and made a beeline for the closing door. "I want to get off here."

The driver muttered something in a tone of disgust about passengers dozing past their stops, but nevertheless reopened the exit door. Calling a sweet-voiced thank-you to the driver's reflection in the rearview mirror, Tina alighted, and not an instant too soon, for the doors swished shut again just as she took a leaping step onto the sidewalk.

Holding her breath, she waited until the exhaust fumes from the departing vehicle had dissipated, then drew in a deep breath of the fresh evening air.

Eric noticed Tina walking toward him when she got to about the middle of the block. Sitting on his bike across the street from her stop, he had been watching for her for twenty-odd minutes. After nearly an hour spent that morning on the phone with his brother, with almost half of it listening to Cameron's drawling-voiced heckling, then sitting all day fruitlessly watching the house across the street from his apartment, Tina Kranas was a delightful sight for his numbed mind and tired eyes.

Of course, with her lovely face and enticing body, the sight of Tina was also a kick to his lately reactivated libido.

Kick-starting the engine, he cruised down the street until he was opposite her, then making a U-turn, he glided up to the curb to keep pace alongside her.

"Hey, lady, want a lift?" he called over the growl of the powerful machine.

Tina tossed him a quick look, then, just as quickly, turned away to stare straight ahead. "No, thank you," she said, in a voice also raised above the bike's rumble. "I'd rather walk."

"All the way to the restaurant?" His question got its intended result—her attention.

Coming to an abrupt stop, Tina swung around to frown at him. "Restaurant?" she repeated. "What restaurant?"

Eric killed the engine before answering. "The one out on the highway with the Colonial name and atmosphere—The Continental Congress Inn."

"But why would I walk all the way out there?" she demanded, her frown deepening.

"To have dinner with me?" Eric answered, in all apparent innocence.

"Dinner?"

Eric couldn't deny the soft smile that teased his lips; she looked so darned cute in a state of bemusement. "Yeah, you know, food, drink, congenial conversation."

Tina sighed and raised a hand to massage her temple. "I have a headache."

Eric suppressed a grin. "I haven't asked you to go to bed with me," he said solemnly, "only to dinner."

She gave him a wry look and slowly shook her head from side to side. "I really don't think..."

That's as far as he let her go. "You're not hungry?"

"Well, yes, but—"

"Please come," he said in a coaxing tone, once again interrupting her. "I made reservations."

Tina stared at him for long seconds, then heaved another, defeated-sounding sigh. "Oh, all right," she said. "I skipped lunch, and I am hungry."

Despite her less-than-enthusiastic acquiescence, Eric felt a rush of elation. Before she had a chance to change her mind, he steadied the bike and leaned forward, making room for her on the saddle. "Hop on," he said, glancing at his watch. "The reservation is for seven, and it's five-to now."

Wryly reflecting that she had reservations of her own concerning the wisdom of her capitulation to his blandishments—and him—Tina shrugged, donned the helmet he handed to her and gingerly mounted the black-and-silver monster.

Surprisingly, the wild ride with the cold wind blowing into her face didn't exacerbate her headache. On the contrary. When Tina dismounted in the parking lot of the restaurant, she was amazed to discover that her mind felt clearer; the throbbing in her temples had subsided to a dull ache.

Unfortunately, though the pain had diminished, the blast of cold air had not eased the inner turmoil Tina was experiencing concerning her unusual response to Eric Wolfe. How could it, when once again her thighs tingled in reaction to being pressed to the warm strength of his body?

Of course, she had only herself to blame, Tina acknowledged, too aware of him behind her as she followed the hostess to a table placed between a window and a large stone fireplace. The crackling fire in the hearth lent both warmth and light to the ambience of the restaurant.

And the place was loaded with ambience, she silently granted, skimming an appreciative gaze around the room, which, though spacious, retained a cozy, homey appearance.

The Colonial decor did not assault the eyes or insult the senses, but rather imbued a soothing effect conducive to relaxation and low-key conversation.

Now if only she could relax and enjoy it, Tina thought, giving the hostess a smile along with her drink order—seltzer with a slice of lime. But relaxing was nearly impossible with Eric sitting so close to her, watching her every move with his striking blue eyes. Feeling his intent stare as if it were an actual touch, she could barely concentrate on the large menu the hostess had handed to her.

"You haven't been here before?" he asked the moment the hostess turned away from the table.

"No," Tina said, raising her eyes from the menu to skim another glance around the room. "Though several of my friends have recommended it to me, I just never got around to coming. It is charming."

Eric nodded his agreement. "Food's good, too." He inclined his head to indicate the menu. "The broiled seafood dinner is excellent."

Tina lowered her gaze to the menu, noting the listed items included with the dinner. "Too much food," she murmured, perusing the column for a lighter meal. "I'm afraid I overdid it with the pizza last night." She glanced up to give him a dry look. "Have to watch the calories, you know."

"Right." Eric ran an even drier look over the portion of her body visible above the table.

"But I do," Tina insisted, smiling in response to his skeptical expression. "I have to be careful, because I love food, especially fattening things—breads, pastries, pizza, stuff like that."

"So do I." Eric looked surprised. "I love Italian bread, slathered with butter. And pizza. And pastries." His lips curved into a self-deprecating smile. "My favorite is homemade lemon meringue pie."

"And mine!" Tina laughed. "And, at the risk of sounding terribly conceited, I must admit that my homemade lemon meringue is the best."

"Better than my mother's?" Eric asked in feigned disbelief and shock.

"How would I know?" Tina demanded, suppressing an urge to giggle. "I've never tasted your mother's."

"It's to die for," Eric said, his solemn tone of voice belied by a devilish grin.

"Well, in that case," Tina rejoined, "I'll take your word on it."

"You're not willing to die for pie?"

"No." Tina lost the battle against the giggle. "Not even lemon meringue."

It was silly, but it was fun.

The realization suddenly struck Tina that she was not only relaxed, but genuinely enjoying herself. Eric's whimsical sense of humor was a surprise, a very pleasant surprise, since it complemented her own.

The waitress arrived at their table with her seltzer and Eric's beer, asking if they were ready to order dinner. Tina chose the soup-and-salad combo, then studied Eric with unabashed curiosity as he struggled with the tough decision of whether to have the seafood or the charbroiled steak.

And Eric was a subject worth studying, Tina mused. With his tall, muscularly lean body, shock of sun-kissed, tawny hair, crystal blue eyes, chiseled features and downright sexy mouth, in looks alone Eric embodied the stuff of feminine fantasies. In addition to his appealing appearance, he had a great sense of humor and his fair share of charm. In total, the man possessed the power to be devastating to an unwary female. But, she concluded, as she was not one of the unwary, she was perfectly safe. She had traveled the male-charm route, she knew every one of the dangerous curves. It was all familiar territory that she had no intention of traversing again.

Eric chose the steak. Rare. A portent of some inexplicable something? Something feral, perhaps?

Dismissing the errant thought as even sillier than their banter, Tina took a sip of her seltzer and decided to indulge her curiosity about her new neighbor.

"You spoke of your mother's pie as if you regularly enjoy it," she said. "Does she live close by?"

"It depends on what you mean by close," Eric replied, moving his shoulders in a casual-looking shrug.

Tina thought his shrug was much too casual looking, and his answer rather evasive. A warning signal flashed through her, causing a sense of unease that banished relaxation. Along with exuding charm as effortlessly as most men sweat, her ex had always been too casual, and definitely evasive. And for good reason. Glen had had a lot to hide.

Tina had admittedly been naive at the beginning of her relationship with her former husband, but she had never been stupid. She had learned her lesson fast and well. She detested lies, and any form of deceit. Now, observing Eric, she could not help but wonder what, if anything, he might be concealing behind an attitude of charm and casual evasiveness.

"I mean close," she replied, determined not to play by anyone's rules but her own—direct and to the point. "In this vicinity."

Eric narrowed his eyes slightly at the hint of sharpness that edged her tone. But he met her steady gaze straight on, and he answered at once.

"Then, no, she does not live close by. She lives in a small town north of here." This time, when he shrugged, there wasn't a casual thing about it. "Sprucewood." He raised his eyebrows. "Ever hear of it?"

"Yes." Tina nodded. "I've never been there, but I have a general idea of where it is."

Eric made a low sound of satisfaction. "Then you should understand what I meant by 'close.' I can get there in a half hour or so on my bike." He smiled. "To me that's close. It's a matter of perception."

"Hmm..." Tina murmured, taking another sip of her seltzer and asking herself if she was being too picky. Yet, while Eric now appeared quite open, she still felt he was reluctant to talk about himself. Why? It was that *why* that bothered her. In her experience, most men not only were willing to talk about themselves, they did so ad infinitum.

Unless, like Glen, they had something to hide.

Her conclusion made Tina uncomfortable, for several reasons. The most important of those reasons was the undeniable fact of the attraction she felt for Eric, an attraction, moreover, that he gave every indication of sharing.

After her crushing experience with Glen, Tina hadn't planned on feeling attracted to, or becoming involved with, any man. At least not for a good long time. Once bitten, and all that. But, most especially, she sure as sunrise had never dreamed of finding herself attracted to a man she couldn't quite trust.

Or was she being not just picky, but paranoid? she asked herself, even if she did have cause for her admittedly suspicious tendencies. Maybe Eric was reticent by nature. Yet the idea persisted that he was hiding something. But what?

"Do you get the opportunity to visit often?" Tina asked, deciding she might as well question him, since she obviously wasn't learning anything questioning herself.

"As often as I can," Eric answered, readily enough. "Which hasn't been too often lately, since the bike hasn't been running too great."

"Well, maybe you'll be able to visit soon," Tina offered in a commiserating tone. "You did say on Friday that you thought you had solved the problem, didn't you?"

"Yeah." Eric grimaced. "But now I'm not so sure." He heaved a sigh. "Looks like I'll be spending my entire vacation fiddling with the damn thing."

"Too bad. This would have been a good time for a visit," she said. "The weather's perfect."

"Oh, well." Eric shrugged. "Mom understands. I call her at least once a week since my father died and she's alone in the house." He smiled. "Even though my younger brother keeps pretty close tabs on her."

"Oh, you have a brother?" Tina said, wanting to keep him talking, now that he seemed to be opening up a bit.

"Three," Eric replied, his wry tone telling her he was wise to her ploy. "But Jake, the youngest, is the only one living in Sprucewood."

"You're the oldest?"

Eric shook his head. "I'm third in the pecking order. What about—" he broke off, as the waitress arrived at their table with their meals. "What about you," he repeated when the waitress finished serving. "Do you have family living in the vicinity—" he grinned "—or close by?"

"No." Tina shook her head. "I have an older sister. She's married to a rancher in Montana. My parents moved to Arizona when my dad retired."

"So you're on your own?" Eric asked, heaping mounds of sour cream on his baked potato.

"Hmm..." Tina murmured, test sipping her soup for temperature. "More or less." Although the soup was good, the potato looked better. "There's got to be a zillion calories in that," she said, frowning at the vegetable.

"That's okay," Eric said, digging in to it. "I'll run it off tomorrow."

"You work out, too?" Tina asked, squashing an urge to beg for a forkful of the steaming potato.

He finished chewing and swallowed before answering. "Yeah, doesn't everyone these days?"

"Just about," Tina agreed, stifling a sigh as she unenthusiastically stabbed her fork into her salad. "From the president on down." She sighed and made a face at the sliver of carrot speared on the tines. "It seems that most folks today derive some perverse pleasure from torturing themselves with exercise and diets."

Eric grinned. "Yeah, but think of the great-looking corpses we'll all make."

Tina laughed. The laughter eased the tension inside her, and she relaxed again. There was even an added bonus from his dry wit; her headache was completely gone.

Four

Tina hurt all over. A fine film of perspiration sheened her body. Her breath came in harsh little puffs. She was tired. She wanted nothing more at that moment than to sit down, or lie down and rest, relax . . . maybe die.

"Lift that leg and kick and kick and . . ."

The upbeat female voice blaring from the TV lashed at Tina. Gritting her teeth, she kicked and kicked, imagining the instructress as the target for her thrusting foot.

"Higher and higher. You can do it!"

Tina narrowed her eyes on the TV screen. The physical-fitness expert was young and beautiful, with gleaming chestnut hair, sparkling hazel eyes, whiter-than-white teeth and a figure to kill for.

Tina hated her. And yet, without fail, she shoved the video into the VCR every Tuesday and Thursday evening and, like now, every Sunday morning, working off the calories accumulated on the days in between.

One oft-bemoaned bane of Tina's existence was the fact that she loved to eat . . . all the wrong foods.

"Now rest . . . and breathe . . . in . . . and out . . . slowly . . . in . . . and slowly . . . and out . . . slowly . . ."

Raising her eyes, as if seeking sympathy from the ceiling, Tina silently cursed the woman, but inhaled...slowly...and exhaled...slowly...and turned her back on the screen to gaze out the rain-spattered picture window.

Still breathing . . . slowly . . . she focused on a russet leaf the driving wind and rain had plastered to the pane. Autumn had finally decided to put in an appearance.

A blur of movement at the far side of the window caught her attention. Her gaze settled on the figure of a man, a tall man, jogging past the house.

What kind of nut jogs in the pouring rain? she wondered, moving closer to the window to get a better look.

The kind of nut who tools through traffic on a roaring motorcycle and devours baked potatoes drowning in butter and sour cream while sipping on a light beer, she reflected, identifying the jogger as her new neighbor, Eric Wolfe.

"Rest period's over, ladies. Now let's get to work on those flabby upper arms."

"You know what you can do with your upper arms, honey," Tina muttered, feeling smug because she didn't *have* flabby upper arms. Nevertheless, since she also didn't *want* flabby upper arms, she reluctantly dragged her riveted gaze away from the elongated form of her neighbor.

He might be a nut, she mused, swinging her arms around in ever-diminishing circles, but nut or not, Eric Wolfe did possess one fantastic body.

Memory flared to vibrant life. The too-peppy sound of the instructress's voice faded into the background. A delicious chill shivered along Tina's spine. The leotard clinging to her thighs seemed to contract, confine, conjure up a response.

She could feel him pressing against her flesh, as he had on Friday morning and twice last night, zooming to and from the restaurant, the slim tightness of his tush and hips a solid presence between her parted legs.

Tina's breathing processes slowed, then raced forward. She was panting, nearly gasping. Her leaden arms fell unnoticed to her sides. Her eyes stared sightlessly at the TV screen. Her stomach muscles clenched. Perspiration trickled in rivulets down her temples and at the back of her neck. She felt drained of energy, weak all over.

"Geez!" Tina whispered, raising a limp hand to massage her nape. "Talk about chemistry!"

The video was only three-quarters over, but Tina knew that she was through for the morning. Drawing a shaky breath, she reached for the remote control and pressed the Stop button, then hit Rewind.

Nut or not, Eric Wolfe was nothing if not dynamic—at least as far as the crackling awareness the mere sight of him instilled in her was concerned, Tina acknowledged.

Eric had played the role of the perfect gentleman when he brought her home last night, even leaving the bike idling in the driveway while he escorted her to the front door, even though Tina had insisted it wasn't necessary for him to do so. He had plucked the keys from her unsteady fingers and unlocked the door for her. Then he had stepped back, not so much as touching her hand as he wished her a murmured goodnight.

Tina had been rendered speechless, and she had been wide-eyed with surprise as she gazed after his retreating figure. After the sensual awareness that had simmered beneath the surface between them all evening, she had expected Eric to make a move on her when he brought her home—try to take her in his arms, kiss her, or at the very least, since it wasn't very late, suggest she invite him inside for a cup of coffee or something.

It was the contemplation of that possible something that had made Tina's hands unsteady. All the way home, she had worried the question of what she would do if Eric did attempt to kiss her...or something. Then, when he hadn't so much as brushed his fingers against hers, Tina had been hard-pressed to decide whether she felt relieved or insulted.

If truth were faced, Tina had to acknowledge that she was more than passingly curious as to how it would feel to have Eric's sexy-looking mouth pressed to her lips.

Of course, Tina had no intention whatsoever of facing that truth. She was too busy reminding herself that the absolute last thing she wanted was involvement with a man.

Now all she had to do was figure out a way to stop speculating about him, banish him from her mind.

Stealing a quick glance through the window over her shoulder, Tina admitted ruefully that ejecting Eric Wolfe from her mind would not be a simple matter. Some masculine essence of him spoke in eloquent and erotic terms to some wayward and errant feminine essence inside her.

Tina felt a hollow yearning, a blatant hunger she had not experienced since the very early days of her marriage.

Wrong. The denial flashed through her mind, bringing with it the unwanted added baggage of self-realization. She had very recently conceded that not even with Glen, before or after they were married, had she experienced such a degree of melting arousal. Not with Glen or any man she had met since her divorce.

Ted immediately came to mind; Ted, and the drunken play he had made when she drove them home Friday night. He had pressured, cajoled, even coaxed her to allow him to deepen their friendship into a more intimate relationship.

Tina had been tactful, but she had been firm, letting him know she simply wasn't interested. And she wasn't, and never had been. Even with her husband, she had pondered her lack of burning enthusiasm for the physical act of love; hadn't Glen repeatedly accused her of being cold, devoid of sensuality? He had. And hadn't she come to accept his accusation? She had.

But that had been before she met Eric Wolfe and her hormones went bananas.

And, except for the odd bits of information she had wrung from him last night, she didn't even know the man.

Tina shuddered. She didn't like it. She didn't want it. She didn't need it.

Well, it had been nearly two years since... and maybe she did need *it*... but...

Both startled and shocked by her own silent admission, Tina forgot the video and took off at a trot for the shower, as if she could run away from her own thoughts.

He had to be nuts. Eric made the conclusion as he stripped the sodden sweats off his chilled body. Certifiable. No doubt about it. Grinning at his rain-slicked reflection in the medicine cabinet mirror, he stepped into the bathtub and under a stinging-hot shower spray.

She looked sexy as hell in a leotard.

Heat unrelated to the steaming water cascading over him streaked through Eric's body. Without appearing to look or turning his head as he jogged by her house, he had caught a glimpse of Tina standing at the wide window, her neat, curvaceous body encased in an electric blue-and-sun yellow spandex leotard. He had very nearly tripped over his own big feet.

So, she hadn't been merely making conversation over dinner when she said she worked at keeping herself in shape, too, he mused, slowly turning the tap, adjusting the water temperature from hissing hot to chilling cold.

She'd be lithe and supple in bed.

A shiver shot down Eric's spine. His imagination took flight. He could see Tina, feel her, her arms clinging to his shoulders, her legs clasped around his hips, her body moving sinuously beneath him.

"Damn." Cursing the near-painful response of his body, Eric twisted the tap, shutting off the gushing flow of water. A frown drew his brows together as he stepped from the tub onto the bath mat and snatched up a towel.

Last night, raw hunger for her had begun gnawing at him at the sight of her tempting mouth, so close and yet so far away across the table from him. He had fully intended to pull Tina into his arms and taste her luscious mouth when he escorted her to her front door, and he would have, if he hadn't noticed the fine tremor in her fingers when he took her keys from her. The impetus to hold her, crush her lips beneath his, had been squashed by the protective feeling that had swamped him. Suddenly certain that Tina was fearful of just such a move on her by him, Eric had backed off, leaving her untouched, unkissed—and, in the process, himself frustrated as hell.

Tossing the towel in the general direction of the hamper, Eric strode into the small bedroom. The visible physical effects of his erotic speculations had dissipated, but his mind had set on a course of action. He needed to work on calming her fear of him; that might be enjoyable. Then he would feed the beast. Sooner or later, one way or another, he was determined to make a feast of Christina Kranas. The sooner the better.

A short time later, his hair still damp from the shower, his lean cheeks close-shave shiny, his body subdued and dressed in faded jeans, a washed-out gray sweatshirt and his favorite, if scruffy, running shoes, Eric stood at the stove, whistling through his teeth as he scrambled three eggs in a shallow frying pan.

When it came to feeding, there were beasts, and then there were beasts. His empty stomach was one of them.

After finishing the meal, Eric took up his position at the window, dividing his attention between the house across the street and the one containing the beautiful object of his increasing interest and desire.

Quite like the majority of residents in the community, the couple living in the house across the street were in their middle thirties. Robert Freeman and Dawn Klinger were both well educated and career oriented. Although they had been together for seven years, they had never legally tied the relationship knot. There were no children.

Which was all rather normal by the prevailing societal standards. Bob Freeman was outgoing, easy to get along with, the type commonly referred to as a nice guy. He was a middle-management employee with a medium-size paper products company located on the outskirts of Philadelphia. Dawn Klinger managed the ladies'-wear department of a local discount store. She was described as a quiet homebody type.

While still married, Tina and Glen Reber had been close friends of Bob and Dawn. And although Tina had withdrawn somewhat after the divorce, her former husband had maintained the friendship, and continued to visit the couple on a fairly regular basis.

Again, all rather normal sounding.

But was it? Eric snorted. He was a veteran of over ten years on the force. He had been around the block, and not just jogging, either. If his hunch, along with the information garnered from one of his informants, was on target, Glen Reber and the couple across the street had deviated from the norm by dabbling in the dangerous business of illegal substances, initially as users, and then as dealers.

And now the word on the street was that there was going to be a very big deal going down soon in the house across the way. Having met Tina, and now wanting her, Eric hoped like hell that she wasn't involved in the filthy business. But, either way, he had determined to be there for the payoff.

It proved to be a long and boring morning. The rain continued to pour from the heavy gray sky. Apart from the leafless tree branches whipping about in the gusting wind, there was absolutely nothing moving in the neighborhood.

Slumped in the one comfortable chair, which he had drawn up to the window, Eric stifled a yawn and shifted position in the padded seat to ease the numbness in his rump. He was settling in again when a black luxury car glided to a stop in front of Tina's house.

"Hel-lo," Eric murmured, sliding upright in the chair. "Look what the wind blew in." He immediately identified the man who stepped from the Lincoln and dashed to the overhang above Tina's front door. "Ah...the former husband and possible suspect, Glen Reber. Interesting."

A picture formed in Eric's mind of the investigative report Cameron had run on the possible suspect. It seemed that Glen Reber was average—height, weight, appearance, everything. Everything, that is, except for a few minor facts, such as the fact that he had a police record dating back to his late teens, and the fact that his lavish life-style didn't equate with his salary—not by a long shot.

Eric had a bone-deep suspicion that Reber was supplementing his legal income with rake-off funds from his association with Bob and Dawn's sideline. That suspicion didn't bother Eric to any great degree; if Reber was walking outside the law, they would nail him, along with the other two.

What did bother Eric was the question of whether or not Tina had her slender fingers in that messy pie.

The boredom of the morning banished by Reber's appearance, Eric sat forward, peering through the rain at the man repeatedly stabbing a finger into the illuminated doorbell button set in the frame of Tina's door.

"All right, all right, I'm coming," Tina called, turning away from the stove to rush to the door. "Give it a rest," she went on in a mutter, shaking her head and breaking into a trot when the bell trilled again.

"Well, it took you long enough," Glen complained when she pulled open the door. "What were you doing?" he asked irritably, walking into the house—uninvited.

"Basting a chicken." Tina gave him a wry look. "Why don't you come in, make yourself at home?"

"I am in." Glen took on what she had come to think of as his lost-puppy expression, all big eyed and sorrowful. "And I wish it still was my home."

If Tina was moved, it was to a knowing smile. "How strange," she said, in an exaggerated drawl.

"Since you spent so little time here when it was your home."

"Don't start that again," he groused.

"I'm not starting anything." Tina conveyed her unconcern with a light shrug of her shoulders. "But I do recall that you spent more time in the various houses of several different women than you ever did in this home."

"Maybe I wouldn't have if there had been a warm and willing body here," he retorted.

At one time, Tina had conceded his point. For though she had never rebuffed his sexual advances, she hadn't abandoned herself to them, either. But that time was long gone, and she was no longer buying his guilt-trip ploy.

"Yes, I think you would have," she said with gentle chiding. "You feed your ego on scoring with other women."

"It's the challenge," he admitted, with blunt and unusual honesty. "They mean nothing to me."

Tina had learned to be as blunt. "Neither did I."

"That's not true." The denial was quick. "You were the only one I ever wanted to marry."

She laughed in his face. "No, Glen, you married me because I posed the ultimate challenge. A, I was a virgin. And B, I absolutely refused to sleep with you in anything other than a bed of marriage."

"Yeah." He sneered. "You were a little prude." A smile of utter male superiority twisted his lips. "You still are. I keep tabs on you, you know." His smile went smooth with satisfaction. "I'm still the only man who ever had you."

"Big deal." Tina made a wry face. "With you I learned that sex isn't all it's cracked up to be."

"You see?" Glen pounced on her admission. "It was that attitude of yours that killed our marriage."

"Whatever." Tina was not offended; she was bored with the subject. "Was there a reason for your visit today?" she prompted, anxious to get back to basting her roasting chicken.

"I'm on my way over to see Bob and Dawn."

She turned to open the door. "Give them my best."

"I want us to get back together."

The hard demand in his voice froze Tina with her hand hanging in midair, an inch from the doorknob. Then she slowly turned to look at him, really seeing him for the first time since their divorce. Glen looked good, attractive, well dressed, properous, sure of himself.

Sure of her? Tina wondered. On the flimsy basis of the fact that she had not been intimate with any other man, did he seriously believe she would even consider a reconciliation after all this time of enjoying her freedom?

Of course, Glen didn't know how much she enjoyed her freedom; his massive ego wouldn't allow him to consider the possibility. What a jerk, Tina thought. What had she ever seen in him?

"Did you hear me?" Glen asked, testily. "I said..."

"I heard." Tina swept his five-foot-ten-inch frame with a dismissive glance. "The answer is no."

"You can't mean that," he said, closing the short amount of space between them. A suggestive smile curved his mouth, and he raised a hand to caress her cheek. "By now, even you have to be needing a little loving."

What he said was perfectly true, Tina allowed, as she had so recently discovered. But she certainly did not need Glen's version of loving, either emotionally or physically.

"My needs, or lack of them, are none of your business," she said, grasping the doorknob and swinging open the door. "Goodbye, Glen."

He looked angry for a moment, but then he flashed her a cocky smile. "Okay, baby, but you don't know what you're missing."

"That's where you're wrong," she corrected him, smiling back at him as he stepped outside. "As far as you're concerned, I know exactly what I'm not missing."

Glen looked to be on the point of exploding. "I'm going. I'll come talk to you some other day." He swung away and started down the flagstone path to the sidewalk, sniping over his shoulder, "When you're not in such a bitchy mood."

"I'll survive the wait," Tina called after him. Slamming the door, she leaned back against it, drawing deep, calming breaths into her constricted chest.

The gall of the man, she railed in silent fury. What she was missing, indeed. She didn't need him...not for anything, and especially not for sex. Pushing away from the door, Tina headed for the kitchen. She was doing fine on her own. She didn't *need* any man, she assured herself.

But she did *want* one particular man.

The unexpected thought brought Tina up short. Standing in the center of the sparkling-clean room, she stared into the middle distance, while gazing inward, examining the wild idea her mental processes had come up with.

Eric Wolfe.

Tina shuddered in response to the flash of excitement the mere thought of him caused inside her.

What kind of lover would he be?

That thought set the excitement to rioting throughout her entire being. Tina could see him, feel him, smell him, his broad shoulders, his slim waist and hips, his long legs, his slender fingers, his masculine, sensuous mouth.

A low moan escaped the sudden tightness of her throat. A fine film of perspiration slicked her forehead. What was happening to her? Tina cried in silent wonder. She had never, ever, reacted to a man in this overheated manner.

Breathing in great gulps of steadying air, Tina raised her hand and drew the back of it across her forehead. She felt odd, strong yet weak, hot yet cold...and needful.

What to do about it? Tina pondered the question. She had options, lots of them. The safest choice being to put all speculative thoughts of Eric Wolfe from her mind.

But was that really what she wanted? Without giving a second thought to the question, Tina shook her head in denial. Her reaction to being with Eric last night, both hopeful and fearful of having him touch her, kiss her, and then the sensations she had felt on seeing him jog past her house that morning, gave ample proof that putting him from her mind was not at all what she wanted to do.

If she was brutally honest with herself, Tina had to admit that what she wanted to do was find out, once and for all, if she was the unresponsive block of ice that Glen had repeatedly accused her of being.

And Tina felt, sensed, instinctively knew, that Eric was attracted to her. If he wasn't, why pay so much attention to her at the tavern Friday night, bother to meet her at the bus stop yesterday?

But, on the other hand, if he did feel attracted to her, why hadn't he made a move on her last night? Tina frowned as she wandered back into the kitchen. Since she had never seriously participated in the male-female ritual games, she was unsure of exactly how to read the signs. For all she knew, Eric was playing it cool, biding his time, waiting for some kind of signal from her.

Okay, she decided, she'd give him that signal.

But how to proceed?

Seduce him?

Tina laughed out loud at the sheer ludicrousness of the idea. She wouldn't know where to begin.

The aroma of roasting chicken wafted to her, stirring her senses with a possible solution.

She could begin by inviting Eric to dinner.

Eric sat, still and tense, watching Tina's house through narrowed eyes.

"Ah..." His breath hissed through his teeth when he saw the door open and Glen Reber step outside. A quick glance at his functional wristwatch told Eric what he already knew; the man had been inside, alone with Tina, for less than fifteen minutes—hardly enough time for any meaningful acts of intimacy.

It was not until that instant that Eric acknowledged the emotions tying his gut into hard knots. He was feeling angry, and frustrated, and protective with regards to Tina and the man who had once shared her bed. But by far the strongest emotion gripping him was a raging possessiveness.

If he should ever learn that Reber touched Tina, in any personal way, he would blow the bastard away.

The decision so shocked and startled Eric, he bolted out of the chair.

What the hell?

Upright, Eric became painfully aware of his hard body condition, and he knew, precisely, what the hell.

All the time he had sat there on the edge of his seat, intently watching her house, Eric had envisioned scenes of Tina, pinned to her bed beneath that slimy creep.

"Only through me, you punk," he snarled at the man now crossing the street. "Tina is mine."

That statement startled Eric every bit as much as his unheard-of feeling of possessiveness. He mulled it over while monitoring Reber's progress to the house across the way.

Tina . . . his?

"Yes." His voice hissed through his teeth once more. On the spot, Eric decided that if anyone was going to pin Tina to her bed, it would be *him*.

Acting on the decision, Eric pivoted away from the window. The trio across the street were closeted away from his sight. Besides, he could keep watch from any location along the quiet street. Detouring past the single kitchen cabinet, he scooped a cup from the shelf.

Eric was going to visit his neighbor.

Five

The doorbell rang.

"Now who?" Tina muttered, pressing the fork tines into the dough edging the pie pan. "If that's Glen again, I'll..." Her voice faded on an exasperated sigh. Setting the fork aside, she turned away from the countertop.

The doorbell pealed once more. Heaving another sigh, Tina shot a helpless look at her flour-speckled hands, shrugged and, tearing off a paper towel, wiped her hands as she marched out of the kitchen, through the tiny dining room and across the living room to the door.

"Darn it, Glen, I'm—" Tina began, as she yanked open the door. Her spate of impatience dried in her throat at the sight of Eric Wolfe sheltering from the rain beneath the overhang above the front stoop.

"Hi, neighbor," he said, giving her a slow, bone-melting smile, while holding a cup aloft for her inspection. "May I borrow a cup of... coffee?"

"Grounds or brewed?" Tina returned his smile, along with an arch look.

Eric's smile evolved into a grin. "Brewed, please, with a splash of milk, no sugar."

"You want it to go or to drink here?"

"You have any cookies?"

"Yes." Laughter gave a threatening quiver at the corners of Tina's lips.

"Then I'll drink it here." He lifted one tawny eyebrow questioningly. "If you don't mind?"

"Do you mind having your snack in the kitchen?"

"No." Eric shook his head. "I come from a long line of kitchen sitters."

"Then I don't mind." Tina gave in to the laughter and swung the door wide. "Come on in."

"Thanks, neighbor."

"You're welcome," Tina replied, observing him wryly as he entered and glanced around the room.

"Nice," he said, turning to watch her shut, then lock the door. "Who's Glen?"

"My ex-husband."

Eric's eyebrow shot up again. "You were expecting him to stop by today?"

"No... yes," Tina floundered, frowning. "He was here a few minutes ago. That's his car out front, the big expensive one,'' she explained, even while asking herself why she should feel a need to do so.

Eric shot a glance through the large picture window. ''He's not in the car,'' he observed, dryly stating the obvious.

''He's visiting friends across the street.'' Tina's smile was as dry as his tone. ''When the bell rang, I thought he had come back for something.''

''Something?''

There was an element contained in Eric's quiet voice that sent a chill down Tina's spine.

''He's making noises about a reconciliation.'' Tina shrugged, to dislodge the cold sensation as much as to dismiss the very idea of Glen's suggestion.

''You're not hearing his noises?'' The chilling element in his voice was gone, replaced by what sounded to Tina like more than mere interest.

The word *interrogation* crept into her mind; Tina dismissed it at once. She had wanted some proof of Eric's attraction to her, hadn't she? she chided herself. Well, what better proof could she ask for than more than mere interest? The conclusion brought the smile back to her lips, and a lighter, careless shrug to her shoulders.

''I stopped hearing him on that topic long ago,'' she said, motioning him to follow as she led the way to the kitchen. ''Come along if you want some coffee.''

''Does this mean the subject of your ex is closed?'' Eric inquired, trailing her through the dining room.

Tina felt a twinge of impatience at his persistence, but squashed it at the optimistic consideration that he just might be feeling a trifle envious of Glen.

"No, not closed," she replied, going straight to the automatic coffeemaker on entering the kitchen. "There's simply not much to say about it, that's all."

Eric watched her in silence as she went through the drill of lining the basket, measuring the coffee grounds and pouring the water into the grate. Tina could feel his steady regard. It made her nervous, in an excited way. She had to concentrate to keep from fumbling the simple routine.

"Was he abusive?"

Tina exhaled an audible sigh as she turned to face him. "If you're asking if he ever hit me, the answer is no," she said, meeting his crystal blue stare levelly.

Eric's smile told her he had heard what she hadn't said. "Verbal abuse, then," he said flatly.

Tina managed to maintain his stare, and her silence, for a few seconds. Then she turned away, moving to the fridge to get out the milk. From the fridge, she went to the food cabinet to remove a package of oatmeal cookies.

"Tina?" Eric's voice was soft on the surface, but held an inner thread steely with purpose.

"All right," she snapped, whirling to face him. "Glen was often less than pleasant."

"As in—" he arched that one tawny brow "—very recently, when he was here?"

The short hairs at Tina's nape quivered at the iciness underlying his too-soft voice. She wasn't deceived for an instant by his bland expression, either. Without knowing how she knew, Tina was certain that Eric Wolfe could prove to be very dangerous when he was riled.

"It's unimportant, really," she said, prudently deciding to do her best not to rile him. "He doesn't stop by often, only when he comes to visit his friends."

"They're not your friends, too?"

"Not really." Tina didn't try to hide the impatience she was feeling; the subject, and his persistence, was starting to get to her. "They were Glen's friends before we were married, not mine. Although we still exchange pleasantries when we see one another, I don't socialize with them." She managed a tight smile. "Any other questions?"

Eric's return smile was easy, teasing. "Yeah. Where's my coffee?"

"Coming up," she said, the tightness smoothing from her lips. She flicked a hand at the table as she walked back to the coffeemaker. "Have a seat."

"You baking a pie?" he asked, inclining his head to indicate the pan and ingredients cluttering the countertop.

"Yes." Reaching into a cabinet, Tina withdrew two gold-rimmed cups and matching saucers.

"What kind?" Eric asked in an eager, hopeful voice.

"Lemon meringue." Tina tossed a grin at him over her shoulder. "And I've got to finish putting it together," she went on, filling the cups and carrying them to the table. "So, as soon as you've had your coffee, I'm throwing you out."

"Can't I help?"

Tina laughed at the coaxing sound in his voice; it was so patently false.

"I'm serious," Eric insisted. "I'm a bachelor, and I know my way around a kitchen. Let me help."

"Doing what?" she asked skeptically.

"I can whip the egg whites while you prepare the filling," he answered immediately.

Tina gave him a considering look. "Well, maybe you do know your way around the kitchen. Okay," she agreed. "But I'm warning you right now, you mess up my meringue and you are in big trouble, mister."

"Deal." Eric grinned at her and reached for a cookie. "Am I going to get to taste this culinary delight later?" he asked, dunking the cookie in his coffee before popping it in his mouth.

"Well, of course," Tina said, sliding onto the chair opposite him. "That's what this exercise is all about."

Eric blinked and paused in the process of submerging another cookie. "What's what this exercise is all about?"

"You tasting the pie," she replied in exasperation. "How will I know if my lemon meringue is as good as your mother's unless you taste it?"

He burst out laughing. "What have you got going here, some sort of personal bake-off?"

"You might call it that."

"I already did." Eric chuckled.

"I felt challenged when you declared that your mother's was the best," she said airily, lifting her cup to take a tentative sip of the hot liquid. "Even though I suppose it won't be a true test of my skill if you help."

"Hmm..." he murmured, munching away on yet another soggy cookie. "I see your point." He washed down the sweet with the last of his coffee, then held out the cup. "Tell you what, give me a refill and then I'll get out of here, let you get on with your thing."

"Deal," Tina said, echoing his earlier remark. Taking the cup, she rose and turned to go to the counter.

"On one condition."

Tina came to an abrupt halt and spun to eye him suspiciously. "What condition?"

Eric's smile was innocent to the point of angelic. "You let me come back later to taste the finished product."

Tina offered him a heavenly smile of her own. "I'll do even better than that."

"Oh?" He raised one eyebrow.

"Hmm..." She mirrored his action. "How would you like to come for dinner?" she asked, then rushed on. "That is, if you like roasted chicken, mashed potatoes with gravy and cranberry-orange relish?"

"Oh, be still my heart," Eric groaned, dramatically clutching his flat stomach. "What time?"

Tina glanced at the wall clock. "Well, it's almost two now, and I still have to bake the pie... say, six-thirty?"

"Six-thirty's fine." He pushed his chair back and stood. "Forget the refill," he said, starting toward the archway into the dining room. "I'll get out of here now and let you get to work."

"All right." Tina laughed at his show of eagerness. "Don't forget your cup."

"I'll get it later. Don't bother to come to the door with me," he said as she moved to follow. He was midway through the dining room when he stopped to call back, "Can I bring anything to add to the meal?"

"Just an appetite."

"Count on it," Eric drawled in response. A moment later, the door shut with a gentle click.

Tina stood in the middle of the kitchen floor, staring in bemusement through the archway into the empty dining room. Nervous excitement shimmered inside her.

Eric was coming to dinner.

The thought jolted her from her trancelike state. She had to get moving. She had a million things to do. She had to prepare the pie and bake it. She had to tidy the house, pick up the Sunday papers, which were scattered on the sofa and the living room carpet. She had to set the dining room table. By then she'd need another shower, fresh makeup and clean clothes—something comfortable but feminine and attractive.

Tina whipped around to get to work on the pie. A sudden realization had her spinning around again and heading for the living room.

The very first thing she had to do was lock the door, because the very last thing she wanted was a repeat visit from her former pain in the neck.

The Lincoln was still there, looking half a block long next to the curb in front of Tina's house.

Eric ran an admiring glance over the gleaming black car as he loped along the walkway to the sidewalk.

The rewards of dishonesty, he thought disdainfully. Rewards not worth the high price tag they carried.

Dismissing the vehicle, he sprinted through the rain to his apartment. Both the rain and the wind driving it had turned cold. A chill shivered to the surface of Eric's body as he let himself into the flat.

A quick hot shower and a change of jeans and sweatshirt and he was back at work, ensconced in the chair at the window. Not a damn thing appeared to be happening in or around the house across the street.

The hours of the afternoon dragged by; Eric staved off boredom with thoughts of Tina, and the excruciatingly slow approach of the evening ahead.

Dinner à deux. Anticipation rippled through Eric, causing a shiver more intense than that brought on by his run through the cold rain. Unlike Friday or last night, there would be no cadre of friends, no other patrons chattering around them, no waiters or waitresses to intrude. There would only be Eric and Tina... and a roasted chicken.

And the man sitting down to dinner with Tina would be Eric the man, not Eric the cop, he decided, surrendering to a sudden, unprecedented desire for normalcy.

What the hell? Eric mused, shrugging. He was officially on vacation. On his own. He was making the rules, setting the parameters for this self-appointed assignment.

And, for the upcoming night, Eric fully intended to ignore the rules and parameters. Gut instinct told him that Tina was innocent of whatever deals were going down in that house across the way.

If, at a later date, his gut instinct proved false, deceived by his libido, and the course of events revealed Tina's involvement with illegal substances, Eric knew he would revert to form, handle the situation in a professional, intellectual manner. But for now, for tonight, he was driven by a powerful emotional fuel, and he knew it.

That knowledge made all the difference. If push came to shove in Tina's case, Eric would step around emotions and do his job. He knew himself to be incapable of anything else.

But until push came to shove, if it did, Eric was determined to follow his gut instincts... simply because that was what he wanted to do.

But Lord, he prayed his instincts were on target, because Tina was . . .

Eric's thoughts were interrupted by the sudden ringing of the phone. He knew who was calling; only one person had the newly allotted number. He picked up the receiver on the second ring.

"Yeah, bro?"

His brother's quiet laughter skimmed along the long distance line. "Hello to you, too," Cameron drawled. "And how are you on this fine autumn Sunday?"

"Fine, hell," Eric retorted, grinning. "It's raining and windy and cold as a witch's—"

"I get the picture," Cameron said, interrupting him. "I also have some information for you."

"On that list of names I gave you yesterday?"

"The very same," Cameron replied.

"Fast work."

"I'm nothing if not industrious." Cameron's lazy-sounding drawl appeared to belie his claim, but then, Eric knew that quite often appearances were deceiving.

"I'm impressed," he said, and in truth he was. "So, what did you come up with?"

"Zilch. *Nada.* Nothing," Cameron reported. "Every name on that list, male and female, came out squeaky-clean. There wasn't as much as one misdemeanor charge in the bunch." He gave a low chuckle. "Believe it or not, we couldn't even come up with a single instance of high school detention."

Eric laughed. "That is about as squeaky-clean as you can get. I'm glad to hear it, though. I liked all of them." Ted came to mind, and Eric quickly amended his statement. "Well, maybe not all, but most of them, anyway."

"You have trouble with one of them?" Cameron rapped out, instantly alert.

"Nah," Eric said dismissively. "At least not in any legal, or illegal, way."

"Ah, I see. A woman."

"My word, you are the perceptive one," Eric said in a fabricated tone of awe.

"You're too overgrown and dumb to be cute, Eric," Cameron rejoined in apparent amusement. "So, you've taken a fall, have you, just like Jake?"

"Jake?" Eric frowned. "What about Jake?"

"You don't know?"

"Dammit, Cameron!" Eric snapped, immediately concerned for the welfare of the youngest member of the brood. "Would I ask if I knew? What about Jake?"

"Seems he's in love." Cameron's drawling voice betrayed his delight at being one up on his younger brother. "The woman's an associate professor at Sprucewood College."

"Well, damn," Eric muttered. "So baby bro Jake's the first of the big bad Wolfes to bite the dust, eh?"

"It would appear so," Cameron said, too wryly. "Jake says he's going to marry the woman."

Though both alerted to and puzzled by an underlying nuance in his brother's initial remark, and his tone of voice, Eric had no time to ponder it for his full attention was snagged by Cameron's follow-up statement.

"Marry her?" he repeated in stunned disbelief. "Did Jake tell you this?"

"No, Mother told me." Cameron's voice sharpened. "Haven't you talked to Mother lately?"

"No, not since I took up residence here," he said. "I was planning to call her this afternoon, but I kinda got caught up in something."

"Does the something have a name?" Cameron inquired in an amused, taunting voice.

Eric grinned at the phone. "Mind your own business, big bro," he taunted back. Then, not only to change the subject, he said anxiously, "Mother's all right, isn't she?"

"She's fine," Cameron assured him. "Practically ready to run out and buy tiny things for her first grandchild."

Eric laughed. "Have they set a date, Jake and—?" He broke off, then tossed a version of Cameron's question back at him. "Does the woman have a name?"

"Sarah Cummings," Cameron said. "Does yours?"

"Goodbye, bro," Eric retorted good-naturedly. "And thanks for the info. I appreciate it."

"Any time," Cameron drawled. "Keep your eyes open, your mouth shut and your guard up, brother," he said, concluding with his usual advice.

"Will do," Eric replied, smiling as he cradled the receiver. There were times, many in number, when Cameron's over-protective, eldest-son attitude was a large pain in the rump, but Eric couldn't deny the feelings of love and caring he always felt when talking to his brother.

Throughout the lengthy conversation, Eric had maintained his surveillance of the house across the street. As had been the scenario for a week now, not a blessed thing was going on over there.

Doubt assailed Eric. Was he on the granddaddy of all wild-goose chases here? Had he bought a pile of bilge from his informant, like some wide-eyed innocent? Was he sitting here, getting numb in the rear, wasting his vacation on erroneous or misinterpreted information?

Eric was not as a rule subject to doubts about how to proceed in any given situation. Nor was he given to questioning his decisions and subsequent actions, which were always based on intellectual consideration, spiced with a dash of instinct. The very fact that he was now indulging in those troubling doubts and questions caused a hollow sensation in his stomach. He didn't enjoy the feeling. Determined to do something about it, he reached for the phone and punched in a number.

At the other end of the connection, the phone rang once, twice, three times. Eric drummed his long fingers against the arm of his chair. The receiver at the other end was lifted on the seventh ring.

"Hello?"

Eric felt a stab of satisfaction at the sound of his informant's voice.

"Could you use a few extra this week?" Eric asked without preamble, knowing the man had a weakness for the ponies and could always use a few extra bucks.

"Yes," the man replied, then went silent, waiting for instructions.

"The intersection nearest to your office building, tomorrow morning," Eric said, then immediately hung up.

Due to the weather conditions, darkness had fallen early. Eric didn't turn on a light, but continued to sit in the darkened room, ruminating while he watched.

His informant hadn't hesitated in agreeing to a meeting, indicating to Eric that either the man was convinced of the validity of his information or his informant was playing games, entertaining himself at Eric's expense. For the informant's sake, and continued good health, Eric sincerely hoped it was the former, not the latter.

Deep in speculation, Eric took only casual note of a truck's headlights illuminating the rain-slicked macadam as the vehicle moved slowly down the street. But his attention became riveted when the medium-size truck turned into the driveway of the house he was watching.

"More company?" he muttered, leaning forward in the chair to peer through the darkness.

The decorative wall light next to the front door flicked on, but the functional trouble lights strategically placed at the four corners of the structure remained dark.

The door on the driver's side of the truck opened, and a short, burly man stepped out of the cab, just as two men came out of the house. Even in the dark, Eric could identify the men as Bob Freeman and Glen Reber.

The three men came together in the driveway, and the short man turned at once to open the back of the truck and disappear inside the dark interior.

"Hmm..." Eric murmured.

Freeman and Reber positioned themselves at the back of the vehicle. A few moments later, the other man appeared, maneuvering a wingback chair toward the opening.

Curious, Eric thought, frowning. A company that delivers furniture in the evening—Sunday evening?

While Freeman and Reber carried the chair into the house, the short man disappeared into the interior again, to reappear once more, shoving another chair into the opening. Moments later, Freeman and Reber returned to collect the second chair. The minute they had it off the truck, the driver jumped out, shut the door and hurried back to the cab of the truck. Before the other two men reached the house, the engine fired and the truck was backed out of the driveway. The truck took off down the street as the men lugged the chair through the doorway.

Altogether, from the time the truck pulled into the driveway until it backed out again, the entire process required less than fifteen minutes to complete. Of course, the rain was coming down pretty hard, so it was perfectly understandable that the men would hustle through the job.

Understandable, yet also curious, Eric mused. Curious because the job would have been made both faster and a little easier with illumination from the four trouble lights. He knew the lights would have made it possible for him to read the lettering he'd glimpsed on the side of the truck as the driver swung it around, out of the driveway.

Dark as it was, all Eric had been able to catch was one word—Acme. Acme. Hell, he thought in disgust, was he on a stakeout or in the middle of a Roadrunner cartoon?

Oh, well, it wasn't much, but it was better than nothing, Eric thought. He reached for the phone directory to begin searching for furniture stores or companies with the name Acme. He had barely started when his stomach growled in complaint against emptiness. Glancing at his watch, he was stunned to see that it was going on seven, and Tina had told him dinner would be ready at six-thirty.

He was going to be late, Eric fumed. But if he hadn't been in a near stupor from boredom, and unconscious of the passing time, he'd have been in the shower or dressing in the bedroom, and would have missed the truck.

Tossing the directory aside, Eric sprang from the chair and dashed into the bedroom. After a record-setting shower, shave and teeth-cleaning sprint, he shrugged into a blue-on-blue striped shirt, stepped into almost-new designer jeans, and then, carrying his shoes and socks, returned to his post at the window.

Eric was watching the house, while sliding his feet into soft leather slip-ons, when the front door opened and Glen Reber emerged. Eric's eyes narrowed on the man as he hurried along the walkway, then turned in the direction of his car... and Tina's house.

Cursing aloud, Eric leapt from the chair, grabbed his jacket from the back of the only other chair in the room and tore out of the apartment and down the outside stairway. He hit the ground running, and as he whipped around the side of the garage the Lincoln's engine roared to life. Checking his headlong rush, he strolled down the macadam drive. The headlights flashed on as the car was set in motion. It cruised past Eric as he gained the sidewalk and sauntered toward Tina's place.

Dismissing Reber, the couple in the house across the street and the puzzle of a Sunday-evening delivery of furniture from his mind, Eric strode up the walk to Tina's door and gently pressed his finger to the doorbell button and held his breath. He was over half an hour late.

Eric hoped Tina didn't open the door with a heavy object in hand, prepared to bean him for ruining her dinner.

Six

"That was great. You're really an excellent cook."

Tina felt her cheeks grow warm with a pleasurable flush at Eric's praise—not that she had needed to hear his verbal approval of her culinary efforts. The proof of his enjoyment of the meal lay in the empty dishes and decimated remains of the bird on the table before her.

No, Tina didn't need verbal confirmation, but hearing it was lovely, just the same. His vocal appreciation of her offering canceled the last lingering shred of annoyance she had felt at his being so late to arrive. Fortunately, the meal had not suffered. The chicken had been moist, the whipped potatoes had been creamy and the gravy had been smooth and unlumpy.

For herself, Tina could not have said whether the meal was good, bad or merely average. She had eaten sparingly, and had barely tasted the portion she served herself. Her meager food consumption had been due not to a lack of appetite, but to the distracting presence of the man seated opposite her at the small table.

Even casually attired, as he was this evening, and had been on the three previous occasions she was in his company, Eric presented a powerful appeal.

Distracting? Ha! Tina thought, trying to collect her thoughts. *Demoralizing* came closer to the mark. Demoralizing as defined by the fact that one look at him and her morals and deep-rooted beliefs were immediately ready to take a flying leap out the window in unconditional surrender.

"Thank you," she finally managed to respond. "I'm glad you enjoyed it." She lowered her eyes, unwitting provocation in the sweep of her long dark eyelashes. The unmistakable sound of his sharply indrawn breath brought her gaze back to his, a frown tugging her brows together. "Is something wrong?"

"Ah...uh, no, of course not." Eric's lips wore a suspicious twitch. "What could be wrong?"

"I don't know, but..." Tina's voice drowned in a sigh, and she shrugged her shoulders, unwilling to pursue the subject in the face of the blatantly teasing smile replacing the twitch on his lips.

"But?" Eric prompted, flashing his perfect white teeth at her.

"Nothing. Forget it." Bypassing the feeling that she had missed something, Tina flashed her own, if not perfect, at least presentable, white teeth in return. "Are you ready for coffee—and the big dessert taste test?"

Appearing to be enjoying himself immensely, for whatever inexplicable reason, Eric sat up attentively, brought his devilish smile under control and gazed at her from laughing blue eyes belying his otherwise solemn expression.

"Bring it on," he intoned in a deep and serious voice. "I vow to be impartial."

Rolling her eyes, Tina stood and began stacking the dishes. "Just let me clear this away first," she said, gathering the cutlery. "Make room on the table."

"Here, let me help." Standing, Eric scooped up the meat platter with one hand, wrapping the other hand around the gathered flatware—and her fingers.

Tina felt certain that the touch of his hand on hers was impersonal and purely accidental. At least she *reasoned* it was impersonal on his part. For her, the sensations activated, the heat generated, by the touch of his skin on hers was all way out of proportion to a simple contact of flesh.

In a word, Tina felt . . . branded.

"No." Tina knew at once that her denial was too strong, too emphatic. Collecting her wits or what was left of them, she carefully slid her hand from beneath his. "It'll only take a minute. I'll do it."

"But I want to help." The glitter in Eric's crystal blue eyes did not reflect his mild tone.

"But it's not necessary," Tina protested, escaping his penetrating stare by beating a hasty retreat. "You are the guest."

"So what?" he retorted, trailing her into the kitchen. "You had all the work of preparing it," he said, following her to the sink. "I can do my part by helping clear it away."

As he approached her, his eyes grazed, then fastened on the pie Tina had removed from the fridge and set on the counter before dinner. "Will you look at that?" he said in simulated awe. "That lemon meringue is picture perfect." He slid a sparkling look at her. "Lord, it's beautiful. Maybe we should have it framed instead of eating it."

Relieved by the easing of the sudden tension that had intensified in the air between them, Tina was more than willing to play along with his nonsense. She pursed her lips and made a show of giving his suggestion serious consideration. "You know, you may be right. Even though it would be a little messy to frame." She paused, as if pondering the possibilities, an impish smile teasing her lips. "I suppose I could spray it with varnish and use it for a kitchen decoration."

"Wrong." Eric laughed. "I can't wait to destroy it." He turned to head back into the dining room. "You start the coffee. I'll finish clearing the table."

The pie was an unqualified success. Eric required two good-size wedges of the sweet-tart dessert before declaring the unofficial contest between Tina and his mother a draw. He was even more lavish with his praise for Tina's dessert than he had been for the first part of the meal.

Again ridiculously pleased by his compliments, Tina fairly floated into the kitchen to rinse the dishes and load them into the dishwasher. It was after the chore was finished, the kitchen spotless once more, that her elation was tempered by a sobering realization.

Dinner was over. The night was still young. She and Eric were alone in the house.

Now what?

If that little, electrically charged moment caused by the casual touch of his hand on hers was an indication, Tina was afraid she knew precisely . . . what.

She still felt shaky inside from the incident, even after the brief respite that had come from distancing herself from him.

At Tina's insistence on completing the job of cleaning up by herself, Eric had made a token protest, then agreeably ambled into the living room after they finished their second cups of coffee. When she returned to the dining room to wipe the table, he had been sprawled lazily on the plush recliner set to one side of the wide front window.

Tina had experienced a sharp pang of longing at the homey, everyday, normal look of Eric ensconced in the chair. He had discarded his shoes and had his stocking feet propped up on the attached footrest, with his nose buried in the sports section of the Sunday paper.

At the time, still under the heady influence of that tense moment and his euphoria-inducing praise, but at a relatively safe distance from him, Tina had heaved a longing sigh and smiled mistily at the comfortably relaxed look of him.

But that was then, and now was now, and standing irresolute in the gleaming kitchen, Tina didn't have a clue as to what to do next. It had been so long since she was actually alone with a man, she didn't know quite how to act.

Memory stirred, rudely reminding Tina of her idea earlier that morning of seducing Eric.

Yeah. Right.

A thrill shot up her spine. Conditions certainly appeared favorable for such a plan of action. Being with Eric, talking with him, laughing with him, before and throughout dinner, had seemed so easy, effortless. Eric had conducted himself like a gentleman…if a slightly devilish gentleman. He had not stepped out of line by word or insinuation.

Her imagination had stepped out of line.

And yet, in all honesty, Tina exonerated herself with the fact that, from the moment she opened the door for him, there had existed a nearly tangible tension humming beneath the surface between them.

The tension was sexual in nature. Tina was absolutely certain about that. Even with her admittedly limited experience, she would have had to be utterly insensitive not to feel and understand the drawing power of the electrical currents of sensual magnetism.

In truth, Tina was not averse to the new and rather exciting sensations. She was still a bit surprised by the surge of feelings, but not nearly as startled by the onslaught as she had been that morning.

She was a female.

He was a male.

Animal attraction.

All very well in theory, Tina reasoned, acknowledging her cowardice in hesitating to join Eric in the living room. But, in light of her overreaction to that flesh-against-flesh moment, how did a relative novice go about learning the rules of the ritualistic mating game, while maintaining a modicum or, at the very least, a scrap of aplomb?

Not by cowering in the kitchen, she thought, ridiculing her timid self. Grow up, Tina. The time has come for one good woman to come to the aid of her latent sensuality. March in there and learn to be...if not bad, maybe a little naughty.

Moving before she could change her mind, Tina straightened her spine, squared her shoulders and strode from the kitchen. Midway through the dining room, she modified her stride to a graceful saunter.

Eric didn't notice. At least he didn't appear to notice. How could he, with his attention semingly riveted to the colorful comics pages? Stifling a sigh, Tina settled into the club chair placed on the other side of the window.

Eric felt her the instant she swayed into the room. The short hairs at the back of his neck quivered in recognition. The fingers that had so briefly curled around hers itched to repeat the experience. His mouth went dry, as it had at the table when she lowered her eyes, innocent seductiveness in the sweep of her lashes.

Innocent?

Lord, Eric hoped so.

Keeping his eyes fastened on the page he no longer saw, he absorbed the hot shivers of awareness arrowing to every nerve, ending in his rapidly hardening body.

Tina.

Her name swirled inside his mind like the sweetest symphony, arousing a deep, never-before-felt ache of yearning in his innermost being. An image of her formed, an alluring vision exact in detail.

This evening, Tina had allowed her hair to flow free. The honey blond mane swept her shoulders when she moved, an enticement to his fingers. She had dressed casually in a cotton knit pullover and a midcalf-length skirt. But there was nothing casual about the effect on his senses of the sweater softly clinging to the enticing upward curve of her breasts and the full skirt gently swirling around her delectable hips and legs when she moved.

Her soft brown eyes beguiled him; her sweetly sensuous mouth brought a groan to his lips. His breath lodged in a tight knot in his throat and his stomach muscles clenched each and every time he glanced at her.

Eric didn't appreciate the feelings. They were too deep, too intense, way beyond a mere physical attraction. And that flat-out scared him.

Hell, when had he ever reacted with such inner disruption to the mere touch of his hand to a woman's soft flesh? Eric didn't need to struggle for an answer. It sprang into his mind full-blown, in boldface letters.

Never.

From experience, Eric knew he could cope with an indulgence of the senses, without losing sight of his mission at any one particular moment. But this...this stirring of the intellect and emotions along with the senses, the sensual, made him feel vulnerable, exposed, *every* moment.

By her very association with the prime suspects in this nasty business, Tina herself was suspect. And, his gut instinct and inclination aside, Eric knew that he was inviting disaster by becoming personally involved with her.

Somebody could get hurt; Eric was beginning to fear that he would be that somebody.

Therein lay his dilemma. How was he to resist the lure of her, when every living element inside him responded to the strength of the attraction drawing him to her?

He wanted Tina with every physical, emotional and intellectual particle of his being. And, for the first time in his professional life, Eric was afraid he was about to embark on a course of action counter to every principle he believed in and stood for.

If he had any common sense, Eric reflected, he'd bolt from Tina and her house until the question of her possible guilt or innocence was resolved. At the same instant, he acknowledged that he had no intention of either listening to or following the dictates of common sense.

He was here.

Tina was here.

Whatever would happen, would happen.

Giving a mental shrug, Eric raised his eyes from the paper to find Tina staring at him, her revealing expression a study of inner confusion, conflict, and unmistakable, extremely exciting, innocent sexual interest.

Innocent?

The question again stabbed into Eric's mind.

Yes, dammit! Innocent, he stabbed back.

There was something...some quality, an aura almost virginal about her. Which, on reflection, considering the fact that she had been married, should have been laughable.

So why wasn't he laughing?

The tension simmering between then crackled, seeming so palpable, Eric felt he could reach out and coil it around his hands, examine it with his eyes.

He smiled at the idea.

Tina returned his smile with an eager hesitancy that, while endearing, held the power to activate his hormones into a frenzy.

"Hi." Eric was amazed at his ability to articulate the simple one-word greeting, considering his mental state and sudden shortness of breath.

"Hi." Tina sounded as breathless as he felt.

"Kitchen duty finished?" Eric rejoiced at his accomplishment of producing three whole words in an entire and complete sentence.

"Yes."

There was a tantalizing quality to Tina's voice that sent shards of excitement piercing through Eric's mind and to the depths of his taut body.

"Would you like to do something?" Her eyes were clear and guileless.

"What did you have in mind?" Eric's smile was slow and seductive.

"A game?"

"Like what?"

"Monopoly?" she suggested.

Eric contained the laughter that tickled the back of his throat. "Uh . . . no."

"Parcheesi?"

Afraid the building laughter would escape if he opened his mouth, Eric responded with a quick and decisive negative shake of his head.

Tina's eyes sparkled with a suspicion-arousing gleam of inner amusement. "Boggle?"

Eric lost it. "Boggle?" he choked out before giving way to the eruption of uninhibited laughter.

Tina managed to maintain an indignant expression for all of fifteen seconds, and then her own throaty laughter pealed forth to mingle with his.

"Okay," she said when their mutual bout of hilarity subsided to an exchange of grins. "What, then?"

Squashing the urge to voice the desire that immediately sprang to mind, Eric swept the room with a quick glance, noting with a surge of satisfaction the stereo components on a table in one corner.

"How about some music?"

"Music?" Tina revealed her incomprehension with a blank frown. "Yes, of course, but—"

"If we shove the sofa back a little," he interrupted her to explain, "we could clear enough space to dance."

"Dance?" she echoed. "Here? Now?"

"Sure. Why not?" Eric said, prudently refraining from telling her the type of horizonal dancing he'd prefer to engage in with her, while consoling himself with the hope of at least holding her in his arms if she agreed to the vertical form of erotic exercise. "I've been wanting to dance with you since Friday night at the tavern."

"But you never said a word about dancing," Tina said, frowning. "Did you?"

"No." Eric grimaced. "Hell, you could barely make your way through that mob, let alone dance." He indicated the floor with a flick of his hand. "In comparison to that floor in the tavern, this is a veritable ballroom." He gave her his most appealing smile. "What do you say?"

Tina hesitated, but only for a moment, and then she shrugged. "Well, all right. What kind of music would you like?" she asked, rising to walk to the stereo system.

The dirty-dancing kind, Eric answered to himself. "What have you got there?" he countered aloud, easing the footrest back into position against the chair, then getting up to attend to the business of moving the sofa.

"Well, I lean toward the classics," she confessed in warning, almost apologetically.

"Do you have any Rod Stewart?" he asked, "Tonight's the Night" in particular springing to mind.

"No."

"Phil Collins?" Eric suggested, holding out hope for "One More Night"...or one night, actually.

Looking woeful, Tina shook her head.

"Well, we can hardly dance to Beethoven's *Fifth,*" he said in exasperation. "What do you have to dance to?"

"I do have some Mantovani."

That stopped him in midsofa shove. Eric blinked, then stared at her in sheer disbelief.

"Mantovani?" he asked in laughter-choked amazement, after long seconds of dumbfounded silence. "My mother and grandmother have Mantovani."

"So do mine. I grew up listening to Mantovani. What's wrong with Mantovani?" Tina demanded. This time her indignance was definitely unfeigned.

"Nothing, nothing, Mantovani's fine," he said soothingly, bidding a sad farewell to dirty dancing. "It's kinda waltzy, isn't it?"

"Hmmm..." Tina murmured, nodding and giving him a droll look. "Violins, you know."

"Yeah, okay," Eric replied, returning his attention to the sofa.

A few moments later, just as he was straightening from the moving task, the strains of "Fascination" swirled in the air. Eric's pulses leapt as Tina waltzed across the cleared floor space and directly into his waiting arms.

Hey, this Mantovani guy's all right, Eric reflected, adjusting his steps to hers. Holding her in his arms was wonderful...even with the inches of space separating his body from her swaying form.

Eric wanted to pull Tina to him, to feel each movement of her body against his, but he fought the urge. Don't rush it, Wolfe, he cautioned himself. She had come into his arms willingly enough, but he could feel her uncertainty in her tense muscles. Take it slow, he warned himself. Don't blow it by coming on too strong.

Deciding his self-advice was excellent counsel, Eric raked his mind for a conversational gambit designed to relax her, ease her obvious trepidation.

"Oh, by the way," he began, struck by sudden inspiration brought on by the reminder of Friday night, "I liked your friends." Excluding Ted, he tacked on silently.

"I'm glad," Tina said, blessing him with a smile that stole his breath, and the majority of his wits. "They're a great bunch, genuinely nice." She laughed; the sound of it went straight to his senses. "Even when they're being idiotic."

"Nothing wrong with a little fun," Eric said, laughing with her. "They're okay." And he knew, he thought wryly, thanks to his accommodating brother. He only hoped that her friends' good character was a reflection of hers.

His voiced approval of her regular companions had a loosening effect on Tina. She readily responded to Eric's expressed interest in her business, laughing with him over her descriptions of some of the more exotic, and a few outright erotic, flower arrangements she had been asked to create.

On the fourth cut of the compact disc, the tempo of the music changed from waltz time to something dreamy. Conversation ceased. Their steps slowed. Eric's arms flexed, drawing Tina's pliant form closer to his own. Surprisingly, even with the considerable difference in their respective heights, her body fit snugly, sweetly, into his.

The violins swelled . . . and so did Eric.

Dirty dancing—of a sort—was possible to the music of a hundred and one strings, Eric conceded, thrilling to the expectant ache.

With a murmured protest against the intimate contact, Tina took a step back.

"Sorry," he muttered, inwardly cursing the too-eager response of his flesh. Gazing down at her, he offered a rueful smile with the apology. "But I really don't have a hell of a lot of control over my body's reaction."

Tina gazed back at him, wide-eyed and solemn. "I know, but then, most men don't."

They had stopped dancing and were merely swaying to the music. The occasional brush of their bodies brought an attractive flush to Tina's cheeks. Heat flashed through Eric. The heat of desire from the tantalizing touch, and the heat of anger stirred by her remark.

"You're an expert on men and their reactions?" he asked in a deceptively cool voice, incensed by the thought of how she had gained that expertise.

"No." Tina's hair swirled with the shake of her head. "But I *was* married to one."

Eric felt slightly stunned by the power of the feeling of relief that washed over him. He was so shaken by the unique sensation he had to draw several steadying breaths before attempting a reply.

"That's right," he said, his hand gliding up her spine to her nape, as if unable to resist the magnetic pull of her shimmering hair. "For a moment, I forgot." He speared his fingers into the silky strands, gently tilting her head back.

"What are you doing?" Tina's voice was soft, a whisper on her trembling lips.

"I'm going to kiss you." Curved over her smaller body, Eric lowered his head as he answered.

"Eric."

"Hmm?" he murmured, brushing his mouth over hers.

Tina gasped, then asked in a breathless rush, "Aren't you uncomfortable?"

"A little," he admitted, once again brushing his lips back and forth against hers.

"But— Oh!"

"But?"

"You're going to strain your back."

"Who cares?" he murmured, preventing further comment by sealing her lips with his own.

Seven

Within seconds, Tina didn't care, either, about anything, except for Eric's mouth moving on hers.

The music faded. The room faded. The world faded.

All that remained was Tina, and Eric, and the unbelievably heady sensations created by one pair of lips in contact with another.

Eric's lips were incredibly gentle in their exploration of the contour and texture of Tina's mouth.

The absence of urgency, demand, in his kiss soothed the flutter of uncertainty that had flared to life inside Tina when Eric boldly stated his intention to kiss her.

Eric held her carefully cradled in his arms. Just as his mouth did not attack, so, too, did his hands refrain from groping, probing, taking liberties Tina had not offered.

Time stood still. Time didn't matter. Time did not exist.

For Tina, existence contracted into two mouths, one instructing, one learning. After an initial hesitation, she eagerly sought the tuition, welcoming the new experience, unrestrained in her response.

Slowly, tentatively, Tina parted her trembling lips in surrender and acceptance of Eric's superior knowledge of the subject matter.

Eric's response was immediate. Unfettered desire blazed forth; sensation after delightful sensation rippled through her, stealing her breath and strength, while conversely filling her being with a newfound power.

Tina's imagination soared on the shimmering wings of sensual awareness, transporting her into a realm of glittering erotic possibilities.

With a suddenness that made her gasp, Eric's mobile mouth sparked tiny shards of pleasure throughout her body, inducing a hunger that would not be denied.

Driven by the rampant force of a sexuality set free of the bounds of self-imposed repression, Tina clung to Eric and gave unbridled expression to the voracious needs clamoring for appeasement inside her.

Tina was an apt pupil, swiftly applying the tenets of her master tutor. Her lips softened beneath the hard pressure of his, her tongue joined with his in a tantalizing duel of parry and riposte, thrust and retreat. When he tightened the fingers he had coiled in her hair, she reciprocated by spearing her fingers into the tawny gold thickness of his. And when he lowered his arm from her waist to her bottom to draw her up and into the curve of his long form, she accommodated him by arching her body into the hard evidence of his arousal.

Eric reacted with a quick sureness that set her mind and senses whirling. While maintaining his hold on her bottom, he slipped his hand from her hair to her back and, straightening, swept her off her feet, literally and figuratively.

His mouth fastened to hers, Eric unerringly strode from the living room and along the short hallway to her bedroom. No words were spoken; none were needed.

Actions spoke louder than words.

Their lips parted to explore closed eyelids, cheeks, ears and jawlines, then returned to fuse together once more, each successive joining more desperate.

Their hands fumbled with buttons, tugged at hems, smoothed material from heated, trembling flesh.

The bed was a bower, a soft haven for their passion-weakened limbs. They fell onto it, into it, with murmured sighs of relief; at last the difference in height was nullified—they fit together perfectly.

Fit together, and yet were not joined together.

Eric did not attempt to overwhelm Tina with proof of his desire and prowess. Displaying another facet of his expertise, he proceeded to seduce her, mind, body and soul.

His hands stroked, caressed, memorized every curve and flare of her soft feminine form, while he murmured exciting sounds of encouragement for her to trace the angles and planes of his hard masculine physique.

His tongue drew a slow, moist trail from her nape to the base of her spine, then lingered to delve into the hollow he found there. In her turn, Tina delicately reciprocated the caress, her tongue dancing along his spine.

His fingers circled her eyes, her mouth, the tips of her breasts and the mound of her femininity, while enticing her to a tactile examination of the outline of his eyes, his mouth, the flatness of his nipples and the silky-smooth length of his manhood.

Inhibitions banished, Tina replied in kind to Eric's every touch, every taste, glorying in every delirious delight derived from sensual play and erotic exploration.

The pleasure went on and on, tension curling, spiraling. Eric's kisses grew harder, hotter, more daring, on her lips, on her skin, on her breasts, on that most secret place on her body, until, writhing, mad with desire for him, Tina cried a plea to him to set her free.

Drawing back, he turned away for scant moments, reaching into the back pocket of his discarded jeans. And then, at last, Eric settled between her thighs, his hair-roughened skin sensuously abrading her satiny flesh.

Tina eagerly lifted to him, rejoicing in the fullness of him expanding to fill the emptiness inside her. With wild abandon, she embraced him with her legs, matching his unleashed passion, riding with him into the fountainhead of bliss.

"Are you all right?"

Eric's low voice intruded into the warm pool of satisfaction enveloping Tina. How long had she been floating inside that shimmering aftermath of ecstasy? she mused. Seconds? Minutes? Hours? It didn't matter, for it had been . . .

"Wonderful."

"Yes, you are." His hand lightly stroked her side from breast to knee; his soft voice caressed her emotions.

She smiled and opened her eyes. "So are you," she whispered, too drained to move let alone speak in a normal tone. "I've never, ever . . ." Her voice drifted away on a sigh of utter repletion.

"I've never, either." Eric smiled with tender understanding. His stroking hand wandered up the inside of her thigh. "Do you think it would be possible to repeat?"

Tina blinked, gasped, then parted her legs for his seeking fingers. "So soon?"

"Crazy, isn't it?" Eric said by way of an answer, lowering his head to her breast. "But there it is." He moved his hips against her thigh to prove his claim.

An instant ago, Tina had wanted nothing more than to drift off to sleep. Now she was wide-awake, aware, aroused, shivering in response to the myriad sensations rioting inside her from the draw of his lips on the tip of her breast and the piercing play of his fingers.

This time there was no hesitancy, no slow ascent into passion. Eric *was* passion, desire incarnate.

His fingers continuing to wreak havoc upon her senses, Eric slipped between her legs, his body taut with readiness, a column of searing fire, igniting an answering flame of wanton hunger deep within her.

And this time he was not gentle; Tina refused to allow gentleness. Grasping his firm buttocks, she pulled him to her, arching her hips high in blatant demand.

"Now, at once," she commanded.

Making a growl-like sound in his throat, Eric bowed his muscle-rigid body and thrust into her, only to withdraw and thrust again, and again.

In the grip of the sudden onslaught of unbearable tension, Tina sank her nails into his flesh, urging him deeper and deeper into her, wanting more and more and yet more of him.

His teeth clenched and bared, his taut muscles quivering with strain, Eric drove himself and her relentlessly, striving for the ultimate pinnacle of simultaneous release.

The harsh sounds of their ragged breaths beat against her ears. Sweat slicked their bodies. And still they continued to hammer remorselessly at one another.

Tina was barely breathing when the gathering tightness inside her pulsed a warning of imminent release. Eric's increased efforts signaled his understanding.

A final breath, a strangled gasp, and then Tina shattered into a million thrilling pieces of cascading completion. At that exact same instant, she heard Eric's cry of triumph, and shared the throbbing attainment of his pleasure.

"Whoa," Eric murmured, levering himself away from her to flop onto the mattress beside her. "That was..." He paused, as if groping for words.

"Incredible?" Tina supplied, dragging quick breaths into her oxygen-depleted body.

"Yeah," he said on an exhaled breath.

"Tremendous?"

"Yeah." He turned his head to smile at her.

"Fantastic?" She smiled back.

"Oh, yeah, in spades." Eric would give her that much, but no more. The experience had been, still was, too new, too intense, too mind-blasting, too never-before.

He would need time, time to think about it later, to ponder the nuances of the emotional and mental effects... if he dared to think about it at all.

Time. What time was it, anyway? Eric frowned and swept the room with a searching glance. His gaze fastened on the illuminated numbers on the digital clock on the nightstand next to Tina's side of the bed.

Tina's side of the bed.

The thought repeated itself in ringing tones inside Eric's head. In thinking about it as Tina's side, was he therefore assuming territorial rights to the side of the bed his exhausted body now occupied?

Eric mentally backed away from that idea—it contained overtones he didn't care to contemplate.

What time was it? Although he had looked, was still looking at the clock, he had not registered the time. Focusing, he peered at the dark red digits.

It read 11:16 p.m. Four hours since dinner.

His stomach rumbled.

"I'm hungry."

Tina had drifted into a light doze. Her eyes blinked open at the abrupt and decisive sound of his voice.

"After all you ate for dinner?" she asked in tones of amazed disbelief.

Eric shrugged. "In case you haven't noticed," he drawled, "I'm a big man."

Pulling a droll expression, Tina skimmed a glance the length of his sprawled body, before coming to rest on the most masculine section of it.

"I've noticed," she replied, in a voice every bit as droll as her expression.

Laughing at the rejoinder he had left himself wide open for, Eric pushed himself upright. His laughter ceased abruptly when he saw her shiver. It wasn't until that moment that he became aware of the cool air in the room chilling the perspiration drying on his skin.

"You're cold," he said, swinging his long legs over the edge of the bed and standing to stretch luxuriously. "C'mon, a hot shower will warm you up."

The look Tina leveled at him was less than enthusiastic. "So would a blanket," she retorted.

Eric gave her his most lascivious smile. "Yeah, but it wouldn't be half the fun."

She shut her eyes and grasped the blanket with one hand to pull it around her shivering body. "I'd rather sleep— Oh! Eric, what are you doing?" she cried as, laughing, he slid his arms under her and swept her off the bed.

Not bothering to answer, Eric tightened his hold on her, to share his body warmth with her, but also because he loved the silky feel of her next to his skin.

"Eric, put me down," Tina demanded, curling her arms around his neck.

Eric caught a rough breath when her reaction caused her breasts to rub against his chest. Savoring the sensation of her nipples poking into him, he carried her into the bathroom. Kicking the door shut, he reluctantly set her on her feet, sliding her body sensuously against his.

"You are a tyrant," Tina said, but didn't protest when his encircling arms drew her closer to him.

"You feel good," he murmured into her hair. "Smell good, too. Like a woman who has been thoroughly loved."

Tina pulled her head back to give him a look of distaste. "You mean I smell like raw sex."

"Yeah." Eric grinned. "Turns me on."

"Big deal," she retorted. "Even with my limited experience of you, I'd say it doesn't take much."

"Now that's where you're wrong," Eric said, looking offended, as he reached inside the shower to turn on the water taps. "I'm not easy, you know," he went on, in a voice raised above the sound of gushing water.

"At the moment," she drawled, blatantly staring at a point below his waist, "I'm forced to admit that you are really very hard."

"And getting harder by the second," Eric confessed, his grin turning wicked. Testing the temperature mix, he coiled an arm around her waist and, hauling her with him, stepped into the tub, beneath the spray of water.

"Eric!" Tina screeched, sputtering as the spray filled her mouth. "Do you want to drown me?"

"No." Eric chuckled and reached for the soap. "I want to lather you... all over."

Tina gave him a militant look. "Okay, but on one condition," she said adamantly.

"And that is?" Eric arched one tawny eyebrow.

Her brown eyes gleamed with inner laughter. "That I get to lather *you* all over."

"You drive a hard bargain, woman, but you leave me little choice." A contrived frown creased his brow as he held up the single bar of soap. "The only problem now is—who goes first?" he asked in a tone of consternation, marveling at the intensity of excitement the silly byplay was stirring inside him—and outside, too, come to that.

"Me." Tina made a grab for the soap.

Eric straightened his longer arms, holding the bar aloft, inches above her reach, laughing while at the same time thrilling to the feel of her wet body sliding against his.

How could this be? he asked himself, confounded by the strength of his body's response. He was thirty-three years old, for pity's sake. After the double workout he and Tina had put each other through, Eric would have thought he'd be flat on his back, physically and mentally exhausted, not stimulated, ready and eager to repeat the exercise.

Yet here he was, renewed life surging inside him with each stroke of his lathered hands on Tina's water-slicked body, quivering in response to the glide of her soapy hands on his aroused flesh.

It was unreal. But it was fun.

The baffling question was...was it the circumstances, the availability of the woman? Or was it the woman herself? Eric had a scary feeling that it was the woman herself.

But, damn, the woman herself felt wonderful, every slippery, slidy inch of her.

Despite the confining enclosure, and the awkward positioning, the pleasure mutually derived from the erotic encounter was bone deep and infinitely satisfying.

"I don't believe this," Tina said in tones of combined confusion and amazement.

Join the club, Eric thought wryly, grasping her waist to lift her from the tub.

"Does kind of blow the mind, doesn't it?" he said, ignoring his own water-slick condition in favor of vigorously applying a towel to her dripping-wet hair.

Tina's reply sounded like mumbled gibberish muffled by the folds of the towel.

"What?" Eric lifted a corner of the cloth to peer at her. "I didn't hear you."

"I said, you are smothering me," Tina groused, yanking the towel from his hands.

"Oh, sorry." Eric gave her his most contrite, ingratiating smile.

Tina was noticeably unimpressed. Tossing a wry look at him, she bent her head and wrapped the towel turban-style around her sodden hair.

Grabbing another towel from the wall-mounted glass rod, he stepped closer to begin drying her body.

She stepped back. "I'll dry myself," she said with daunting asperity. "I'd rather you didn't touch me."

Now that really did blow Eric's mind. Unmindful of the runnels of water dropping off his body to soak the bath mat, he stared at her in sheer disbelief, not only of her statement, but also of the searing pain of rejection he felt in reaction to it. "Are you serious?" he demanded. "How can you say that, after the last several hours we've spent together?"

"I can say that *because* of the last several hours we've spent together," Tina retorted. "Knowing what drying each other could lead to," she went on, "I'm not at all certain I could survive another *episode* with you."

"Wear you out, did I?" Eric grinned, suddenly feeling good—no, terrific—and famished.

"Well, actually, yes," Tina admitted, slanting a sparkling look at him.

"Wore myself out, too," he confessed, chuckling. "And worked up an appetite, as well."

"So did I." Tossing the towel into the wicker hamper in the corner, she walked out of the room.

"What do you have to snack on?" Eric asked, dropping his towel on top of hers before trailing after her. "Was there any chicken left?"

"Some of the white meat," Tina answered absently, pulling on a quilted robe. "Might stretch to two sandwiches," she mused aloud, slipping her feet into fuzzy mules before walking to the vanity table to brush her hair.

"You have lettuce and tomatoes?" Eric asked, stepping into his jeans.

"I think so." Tina frowned at her reflection in the mirror. "I should blow-dry my hair," she muttered, tugging the brush through the long, wet strands.

Eric finished shrugging on his shirt, stepped sockless into his shoes, then headed for the door. "I'll make the sandwiches, you do your hair thing." Whistling softly, he started ambling toward the kitchen, only to pause to call back to her, "You want the works, Tina?"

"Sure," she called back to him. "If I'm going to stuff my face after midnight, I might as well go all the way."

All the way. The tail end of her remark replayed inside Eric's head as he gathered the ingredients and began making their sandwiches.

The words from the song of the same title came to him, and he sang them beneath his breath while he buttered four slices of bread, then slathered them with mayonnaise.

"All the way. All the way," he softly sang the song's ending, staring into space, the sandwiches half made.

Tina had gone all the way with him tonight, Eric reflected, frowning at the tomato he held in one hand and the slicing knife he was holding in the other.

She had given herself to him freely, unconditionally, in complete and sweet surrender. A memory chord of response tingled down Eric's spine.

He had set his sights on Tina, deciding he would have her, very soon after their first meeting . . . which he had coolly and deliberately orchestrated.

Yet he had not taken her, but had joined with her; he had not made love to her, but had made love with her. Eric understood and acknowledged the shadings of difference between the two concepts. The first represented greedy self-gratification, the second a desire to share caring, as well as pleasure.

Absently slicing the tomatoes, Eric finished making the sandwiches, then rummaged through the cabinets, hoping to find a bag of potato chips, while mulling over the possible ramifications of his deductions.

He cared for Tina. Really cared for her, Eric realized. He cared for her in a way that could, he feared, very quickly become meaningful.

A sobering thought. One that—

"Snack ready?" Tina asked, ending his reverie, as she walked into the kitchen.

"Yes," Eric answered, relieved at having his uneasy train of thought derailed.

"Good. You want seltzer water or milk?"

"Milk." Eric turned to smile at her, and felt his breath catch painfully in his throat. With her hair a shining golden halo around her freshly scrubbed face, the innocent look of her did more than rob him of breath. It had the strangest, ache-causing effect on his heart.

"What are you looking for?"

"Huh?" he asked . . . like a clod.

Her smile was gentle, increasing the ache in his heart. "I asked if you were looking for something in particular in the cabinets."

"Oh, yeah. You have any chips?"

"Three cabinets down," she instructed.

The chips were found, and swiftly dispatched, along with the sandwiches and several glasses of milk. Tina brought up the subject of sleeping arrangements while they worked together clearing away the debris.

"Ah . . . hmmm . . . are you, uh . . . thinking of staying the night?" she asked, quickly turning away, ostensibly to stash the milk and mayo jar in the fridge.

"May I?" Eric replied, hopefully.

Tina hesitated; Eric held his breath. "You may as well," she said, unknowingly allowing him to live by allowing him to breathe again. "If you want to."

"I want to," he said. "I want to sleep with you, wake up with you." Eric caught himself just in time before adding *every night for the rest of my life.*

Tina turned to look at him, her brown eyes soft, her smile tremulous. "I want to sleep with you, too."

Eric felt like whooping. He didn't. Instead, he forced himself to be practical. "What time do you have to get up in the morning?"

"Around seven-thirty."

"That's a good time for me, too," Eric said, recalling his appointment with his informant. "I have to go into town early, so I can drop you off at the shop."

Tina shook her head. "The shop's closed on Mondays, but I still want to get up early. I can get my car from the garage anytime after they open at eight."

"Okay." Eric shrugged. "I'll drop you at the garage before I go into town."

His stomach was full. The kitchen was clean. The hour was late. He held out his hand to her.

The temperature in the bedroom felt to be somewhere around forty degrees or so. Goose bumps prickled Eric's skin as he shucked out of his clothes. Tina, on the other hand, appeared unconcerned with the cold. A wry smile tickled his lips when she removed the quilted robe. She had not only dried her hair while he made their snack; she had also slipped into a long-sleeved, high-necked, voluminous flannel nightgown—the kind his grandmother favored.

"I was chilly," Tina said defensively.

"Uh-huh," he murmured. "Are you actually going to sleep in that tent?"

"Yes." She said, lifting her chin defiantly. "Do you have any objections?"

"No." Eric grinned. "It is your bed."

"And I intend to *sleep* in it."

"I hear you," he said, his grin dissolving into soft laughter. "I'm not...er, up to anything else, anyway. That is, anything more than a good-night kiss." He arched a quizzing eyebrow. "Okay?"

"Okay." Tina's lips twitched.

In a concession to her sudden modesty, Eric crawled into bed beside her wearing his briefs. The good-night kiss they shared was short in duration, but oddly tender and comforting. The instant their lips parted, Tina whispered good-night and turned onto her side, her back to him.

Eric lay on his back, contemplating their kiss, his shoulders and chest exposed to the chill air. A shiver had him reaching for the blankets, tugging them up to his collarbone.

He was sleeping with a suspect.

The thought jarred him from his reverie. Some undercover cop you are, Eric chided himself. Turning to her, he curled his arm around Tina's waist and curved his body into the warmth of hers, spoon-fashion.

Well, hell, he definitely was a cop, he mused around a wide yawn, snuggling closer to her pliant body. And he certainly was undercover... or covers, as it were.

Eight

"Dinner?"

"Fine," Tina answered calmly, repressing an impulse to leap into the air and shout, *Yes, yes.*

"Are you in the mood for anything in particular?" Eric's voice again sounded disembodied coming from behind the black helmet. "Italian, Chinese, Greek?"

Tina removed her own helmet and ruffled her flattened hair. "No. Are you?" she asked, handing the helmet to him, then smoothing her palms down her wool slacks.

"Seafood," he said, balancing the bike between his thighs as he turned to fasten the helmet to the saddle. "Lobster tail, and maybe a dozen or so steamed clams to start." He turned in time to catch her smile. "Let's not go through that routine again about my appetite," he warned, amusement evident on his voice. "Does a seafood restaurant meet with your approval?"

"Yes." Tina gave her smile free rein, just out of sheer good spirits. "What time?"

"Six too early?"

"No, six is fine," she said, reluctantly raising her admiring gaze from his muscular legs to his tight butt to his slim waist to his broad chest and shoulders and up to the dark mask concealing his expression from her.

"Knock it off." Eric's voice was low, rough edged, revealing his response to her visual evaluation of his physical attributes. "I've got to get moving, and you've got to get your car." He indicated the repair shop behind her with a movement of his head. "I'm going to let you chauffeur for me this evening."

"How kind of you," she drawled, surrendering to the laughter bubbling inside her.

"Yeah, ain't it?" Eric's muffled laughter mingled with hers. "I'm a real sweet guy."

"Your modesty underwhelms me," she gibed, swinging around and heading for the repair shop. "See you at six," she called over her shoulder. *"And drive carefully."*

"I always do," he called back to her on a note of inner laughter.

Oh, sure, Tina thought, wincing as he roared away from the curb and down the road. She suffered a few moments of anxiety for his safety as she recalled the harrowing ride he had given her on Friday morning, weaving in and out of the rush-hour traffic. Then, on deeper reflection, she also recalled his expertise in handling the monster machine and she relaxed.

The car was repaired and ready for her. Tina was feeling so good, so lighthearted, she didn't even balk at the sizable bill the mechanic presented to her. Smiling serenely, she wrote a check, handed it to him, claimed her car and, humming softly, drove away.

Not at any time did the tires leave the road. And yet, riding the winds of euphoria, Tina felt as if she were soaring, the car's tires cushioned by fluffy pink clouds.

It was a lovely sensation, heady and warm. Tina didn't even feel the bite of approaching winter in the stiff autumn breeze that had pushed yesterday's storm clouds away.

The sunlight was weak but glaring, sparkling on the rain-washed air. Tina was sparkling, too. A casual observer might have concluded that she was in love.

Tina herself had not as yet arrived at that earth-shattering conclusion. She felt good. She felt happy. She felt deliciously satisfied, emotionally and physically.

Eric sat on the rumbling but motionless bike, one foot propped on the curb, his watchful expression hidden behind the dark visor. The center-city morning traffic inched past him on the street, while the pedestrian horde surged by him on the sidewalk.

From his position a quarter of a block away from the intersection, he searched the crowd for the familiar figure of his informant. When he spotted the man, Eric lifted his foot and moved the bike forward along the curb, timing his movement to coincide with the man's arrival at the corner.

The contact had the innocent appearance of a driver requesting directions.

"What's the word?" Eric muttered, glancing around, as if thoroughly confused.

"There's been one small shipment," the informant said, raising an arm and pointing, as if indicating his verbal directions. "I hear the demand for more is high, and that there'll likely be one or two more small shipments before the big one's delivered."

"Thanks." Eric extended his right hand, slipping several bills into the informant's palm.

"I'm sure you'll have no trouble now, sir," the man said in a louder voice.

The traffic light flicked to green; Eric waved his hand in a quick salute, then gripped the handlebar and shot through the intersection.

Ten minutes later, Eric drove the bike down the ramp to the underground parking garage beneath a large apartment complex, and brought it to a stop in the two feet of space between the wall and the front bumper of his midsize car. Venting his frustration by kicking the stand into place, he strode to the elevator and rode it to the fourteenth floor.

All the while, his informant's words replayed in his mind: *Before the big one's delivered.*

Delivered.

Delivery.

Damn, Eric fumed, letting himself into his one-bedroom apartment. He'd known there was something fishy about that furniture delivery on a Sunday night.

Too bad he hadn't been able to get the license number on that truck, Eric railed in disgust. Because he'd be willing to bet a ten-spot against a plugged nickel there'd be no listing of an Acme Furniture Co. in the directory.

It didn't take long to confirm his suspicion. There were listings for Acme Dry Cleaners, an Acme Siding Company, Acme Markets, but no Acme Furniture.

Big surprise, Eric thought wryly. Setting the directory aside, he sat staring out the wide window, not seeing the panoramic view of the art museum and the distinctive buildings on boathouse row along the river.

The informant had guessed that there would be at least one, maybe two, small deliveries before the big one.

How big? Eric wondered, adrenaline surging through his system. He had been right to take a flier on this tip, and he'd be there to intercept the big one. All he had to do was wait them out, extend his vacation if necessary, but wait them out. The haul would be worth the wait.

Deciding that after the next delivery he would call his superior and invite him in for the kill, Eric grunted with satisfaction and pushed the button on his answering machine to replay the tape.

There were a couple of messages from friends, demanding to know what hole he had disappeared into, then one from his mother. Unlike the commonly held stereotype of the complaining parent, Maddy Wolfe never whined about being ignored. A smile erased the grim set of his lips as he listened to his mother's brief, directly-to-the-point message.

"Eric, assuming you are still alive, since I haven't heard anything to the contrary, will you give me a call within the foreseeable future? I have some good news."

Laughing softly, and deciding it was in all probability now the foreseeable future, Eric reset the machine then picked up the receiver and dialed his mother's number. Maddy answered on the fourth ring.

"Hello?"

"Hi, beautiful," Eric drawled. "It's me, Eric, your still-alive offspring."

"Gosh, I'm so glad you told me," Maddy said, matching him drawl for drawl. "I'd have never guessed."

Eric absolutely adored his mother. In his admittedly biased opinion, Maddy was the most with-it woman he knew. And he loved the rare occasions when he already knew a juicy piece of information before she could tell him herself.

"Does the good news you mentioned have anything to do with Jake's love life?" he asked, too casually.

"Oh . . ." Maddy said on an exhalation of consternation. "You too? When did you talk to Cameron?"

"Yesterday," he answered, frowning. "And what do you mean, me too?"

"I had a call from Royce not a half hour ago," she said, which explained everything.

Eric laughed. "Big bro stole your thunder, did he?"

"Doesn't he usually?" she asked rhetorically. "I swear, that brother of yours is more a mother hen than I am."

"Yeah," he agreed, grinning. "The Lone Wolfe does keep pretty close tabs on all of us." His grin gave way to a chuckle. "Makes you feel all warm, and cared for, and protected, and even . . . henpecked at times."

"Now, Eric," Maddy said reprovingly. "Cameron's only looking out for our best interests."

"I know, I know. And I appreciate it . . . even if it does get a bit wearing now and again." Deciding it was time to change the subject, he referred to the intent of her message. "So, little Jakey's in love, is he?"

"Well, if he isn't, Jake is certainly giving a good impression of a man in love," Maddy replied, amusement evident in her voice. "And Sarah is a lovely woman."

"Like her, do you?" Eric asked purposely, knowing his mother's knack for reading a person's character.

"Very much," she answered at once, saying much more than she had actually said. "And I believe that you, Royce and even Cameron will like her, too."

"Whoa, lady, are you speaking about the same female-hating Cameron I know and tolerate?"

"Oh, Eric, really!" Maddy exclaimed with a hint of maternal exasperation. "Must you be so cynical? Cameron does not hate females, and you know it."

"No? Could've fooled me," Eric said dryly. "And if I'm cynical . . . well, I've earned the right."

"Maybe it's time for you to transfer to another department on the force," she suggested gently.

"Not just yet, Mom," he said, thinking about the delivery truck that had visited his neighbors on a Sunday night. "But maybe in the foreseeable future," he went on, thinking about the loving warmth of another, blond and beautiful neighbor.

"I hope so, son." Maddy's sigh was soft, but Eric heard it. "Any police work is dangerous, I know, but undercover narcotics is especially—"

"I gotta go, Mom," Eric interjected, gently but firmly cutting her off.

"I'm sorry," Maddy murmured. "I do so dislike a nagging female. But I am still a mother."

"The best," Eric assured her. "I really have to go now, Mother. But I'll be up to see you soon."

"All right," she said. "Let me know in advance, and I'll bake a lemon meringue pie."

"It's a deal," Eric said, thinking that if he wasn't careful he'd have lemon meringue oozing out of his ears. "Take care, Mom. I love you."

I love you.

The phrase came back to haunt Eric off and on throughout the morning, but not in a familial way. Oh, without doubt, he loved his mother and his three brothers, but the phrase playing hide-and-seek with his mind had, chameleonlike, metaphorically changed into a different shade of love.

Tina. Her name whispered through his mind.

Tina of the honey blond hair and soft brown eyes and enticing sweet lips. Tina of the quick humor and throaty laughter and old-fashioned but nice musical preferences. Tina of the warm body and hot kisses.

Damn, Eric mused, just thinking about her made him feel all hot and bothered, weak and strong, possessive and protective, tender and fierce.

Was that love?

Eric honestly didn't know, because he had never been in love. He had been in deep like, but he had never before believed himself in love...except with the blue-eyed, raven-haired minx who'd sat at the desk next to his in the fourth grade, and that didn't count.

So then, Eric quizzed himself while riding the elevator to the apartment lobby to collect his mail, did the warm and wonderful feelings he experienced merely thinking about Tina denote the presence of that elusive, indefinable emotion called love?

Eric reflected on the question on the return trip to his apartment, and came to the conclusion that, in all truth, he simply didn't know the answer.

Putting speculation aside, he riffled through his mail, which mainly comprised bills and junk. And he kept further introspection at bay while writing out the necessary checks to cover the bills.

But even as he affixed the required postage to the last envelope the question returned to haunt him.

Was he, could he possibly be, in love with Tina?

Probing his emotional feelings was not one of Eric's usual practices. But unless he did a little psyche-digging, examining the available evidence, as he would have in relation to his police work, how else could he form an intelligent opinion?

Eric shot a glance at his watch; it read 10:28. Okay, he thought, he'd allow himself one hour of contemplation, but then he'd have to get moving, because, since Tina was not working today, he had promised himself the treat of having lunch with her.

Hell, if truth be faced, he had kind of promised himself the treat of *having* her for lunch, Eric recalled, growing warm all over at the possibility.

There was a clue there, he mused. A bit of evidence for him to examine. Despite the rigorous workout he and Tina had engaged in last night, Eric acknowledged, his passion still ran hot and wild, and his desire for her was unsated.

A frown of concentration creasing his brow, Eric got up and went into his bedroom to collect the suit, dress shirt, tie and shoes he wanted to wear for dinner. While he was arranging the clothes in a garment bag, another clue swam to the surface of his consciousness.

In addition to his strong physical reaction, Eric had to admit that he genuinely liked Tina as a person, despite the unpalatable fact that he still had no definite proof either way concerning her involvement in this drug business.

All of which left him where?

Looping his index finger through the hook and slinging the garment bag over his shoulder, Eric left the bedroom, and then the apartment. Striding along the hallway to the garage elevator, he concluded that, all things considered, if his feelings were a true reflection of his emotional status, he could be in very deep trouble.

Eric felt a sinking sensation unrelated to the swift descent of the elevator. The sensation warred with the anticipatory feelings simmering inside him.

After all these years of unencumbered, uncomplicated, uninvolved bliss, why had he gone and fallen for a suspect, of all females?

The question popped into Tina's mind later that morning. She was stripping the sheets from her bed, dreamily reliving the delightful education in erotic play she had experienced there, when the idea struck.

Was she in love?

Giving a sharp shake of her head, as if to dislodge the ludicrous thought, she gathered the bedding and carried the bundle into the laundry room.

But the seemingly simple question was not so easily banished. Throughout the day, at odd, unexpected moments, it wormed its insidious way to the forefront of her consciousness, insisting she recognize its presence.

In love?

It was suddenly there while Tina was vacuuming the bedroom carpet.

In love?

It whispered through her mind while she was cleaning the bathroom.

In love?

It danced into her thoughts while she shoved the sofa back into place in the living room.

Love!

It finally ambushed her when she paused in her flurry of housework, clanging like a bell inside her mind as she stood irresolute in the kitchen, trying to decide whether she wanted soup or a sandwich for lunch.

Tina knew when she was beaten. Surrendering to the nagging persistence of her consciousness, she considered the euphoria-dousing question of love.

How could she be in love? Tina demanded of herself, dropping like a stone onto a chair. She hardly knew him.

Tina squirmed in the chair, suddenly uncomfortable with the fact that she had willingly made love with, slept with, a man she knew almost nothing about.

She didn't even know what Eric did for a living, Tina reminded herself. All he had said was that he was on vacation leave; Eric had never specified from what type of employment he was on vacation. For all she knew, he could be anything from a corporate CEO to a cat burglar. Tina frowned, made even more uncomfortable by her last thought.

Did cat burglars take vacation leave? Tina wondered vaguely, the distracted thought indicative of her growing sense of unease with the subject matter.

Recognizing the mental ploy for what it was—an attempt to dodge the issue at hand—Tina determined that at the first opportunity she would question Eric directly about his employment. Then she sternly told herself to get it together and get to the point.

The point, of course, being: Was she in love?

Tina sighed, but forged ahead with the self-examination. She had been in love once, and what she was feeling now in no way resembled the feelings she had had for Glen Reber... at least not the feelings she had experienced after the intimacies of their wedding night.

Tina shuddered in remembrance.

Although it was true that there were similarities between the only two men she had ever been intimate with, Tina felt positive that those similarities were few and strictly superficial. Both men were physically attractive, even though, to her eyes, Eric was definitely the handsomer of the two. And they both possessed a certain charm and style.

But that was where the similarities ended. Tina knew from experience that Glen was shallow, unfaithful and often, deliberately cruel. Instinct, intuition, something, made her certain that Eric possessed the opposite qualities, that he was deep, abiding and gentle.

And Eric was one magnificent lover, the inner voice of satisfaction whispered.

Of course, again, Tina acknowledged the irrefutable fact that her only basis of comparison was her former husband. But, she thought, it sure didn't take the intellect of a rocket scientist to arrive at a judgment concerning the differences between the two men in that regard.

While engaged in the intimacy of lovemaking, Glen Reber had proved to be selfish, demanding, ungiving and, when thwarted in any of his desires, sadistically inclined.

In sharp contrast, while making love, Eric had displayed a fiery passion, generating intense erotic excitement, while at the same time conveying a gentle caring, a tender concern and a genuine desire to give pleasure, as well as to receive it.

On reflection, Tina reversed her original assessment; in actual fact, there were no comparisons between the two men. To her regret, she knew that Glen's charming persona was a sham, a mask he donned and discarded at will, to suit his purposes at any given moment.

On the other hand, Tina felt positive, to the very depths of her soul, that Eric's charm, humor and caring style were not in the least surface facades, but were instead integral facets of his true personality.

And she trusted him implicitly.

Tina's sudden realization of the extent of the trust she felt for Eric gave her the answer to her own question.

She *was* in love with Eric Wolfe.

But having the answer did not automatically ease the weight on Tina's mind. She didn't want to be in love—with Eric or any other man. She had allowed herself to be swept away once before by that emotional whirlwind. The aftereffects of disillusionment and pain were devastating, and not worth the transitory thrill of the brief, giddy ride.

So...what to do? Tina asked herself, frowning at the package of luncheon meat she held in her hand, and wondering when she had left her chair to walk to the fridge.

Heaving a despairing sigh, Tina shoved the package back into the fridge; she wasn't hungry for a sandwich. Come to that, she mused, returning to the chair, after gnawing on her unpalatable emotional state, she wasn't hungry, period.

What to do? The new question replaced the old in Tina's mind, goading her into contemplation of her situation, and the options available to her.

She could stop seeing Eric, nip their tenuous relationship in the bud before it had sufficient time to blossom into something infinitely more serious, thus avoiding the possibility of being hurt again, more deeply than before.

Tina pondered the consideration for a moment, then shook her head. What would distancing herself from Eric prove? She would still love him, and the separation would very likely hurt as much as it eventually would if Eric turned out to be as false and insincere as Glen had been.

Getting restless, Tina deserted the chair to pace in a circle around the table. Another, less wrenching alternative would be to continue seeing Eric, but only contingent upon the understanding that their relationship reverted to one of platonic friendship.

Fat chance!

Tina grimaced at the immediate and derisive inner response, but was forced to accept the validity of it. All Eric had to do was look at her and she became all warm and squishy inside. All he had to do was smile at her and her resistance dissolved.

Well, so much for options, Tina thought, figuratively throwing up her hands in surrender. Besides, she didn't want to stop seeing him, being with him, sleeping with him. Simply because she not only loved Eric, she *liked* him.

Even though Eric had not mentioned one word about either loving or liking her.

Tina soothed the sting of that painful truth with the rationale that men in general were always hesitant about revealing the depths of their emotions. It appeared to be a built-in species thing.

Feeling exhausted by her spate of introspection, Tina decided a shot of caffeine was in order. She had scooped the grounds into the basket and was in the process of running cold water into the glass pot when the doorbell rang.

Tina glanced at the dining room archway, then back at the pot, determining to ignore the summons. The bell rang again. Thinking it might be the mailman with something she had to sign for, she turned off the water, set the pot aside and took off at a trot for the door.

It wasn't the mailman.

"Hungry?" Eric asked, brandishing a brightly patterned red-and-white cardboard bucket with one hand and a matching paper bag with the other.

"Yes," Tina answered, her appetite restored by the sight of him. She raised her eyebrows as she stepped back to let him enter. "What have you brought?"

"Chicken wings, hot and spicy," he said, giving her a lascivious grin, along with the bucket. "And mashed potatoes, gravy and biscuits." He held the bag aloft.

Tina's mouth watered and she groaned. "All low-cal, low-fat stuff," she observed wryly.

"Aw, c'mon, live it up," Eric said, handing the bag to her and shucking off his jacket.

"That's easy for you to say," she muttered, sweeping a glance over his lean body. "You don't have to worry about every morsel you put in your mouth."

"Maybe not, but I've got the solution to your problem." He grinned again, more suggestively than before. "We can work it off with vigorous exercise this afternoon." His expression left no doubt about the type of exercise he had in mind. "And if that doesn't ease your cal and fat worries, you can have broiled fish and a salad for dinner."

"I planned to, anyway," Tina retorted, excitement flaring inside her as she led the way into the kitchen. "And it's a good thing, too," she said, prying the lid from the bucket and sniffing appreciatively at the spicy aroma wafting from inside. "This smells wonderful, like an automatic ten pounds to the hips."

As it turned out, the food was tasty.

The afternoon exercise was delicious.

Although Tina still didn't know what Eric did for a living, she did know he was well versed in the art of lovemaking.

She soothed her conscience and excused her lapse by assuring herself that a good opportunity really hadn't presented itself; Eric had kept her rather distracted.

Nine

The opportunity was at hand.

Eric was replete, from the afternoon's endeavors and from the enormous seafood dinner he had consumed. Relaxed, he lounged back in his chair and smiled at her over his coffee cup.

Tina seized the moment. "How much longer will you be on vacation?" she asked, casually lifting her own cup to her lips to blow on the steaming liquid.

"This week...officially," Eric replied, readily enough. "But I could extend it another two weeks—" he smiled with obvious sensuality "—if I wanted to."

"You have four weeks' vacation a year!" Tina exclaimed, grateful for the opening he had given her.

"What are you, the president of a bank or something?"

"Not hardly," Eric drawled. "I work for the city."

"Philadelphia?"

"Uh-huh." He nodded.

"You must have some position." Tina couldn't imagine him in the role of a clerk, pushing papers behind some license-applications counter. "Appointed?"

"Naw, nothing so exalted." Eric laughed. "I'm just a city employee, with the option of using my accrued vacation time all at once."

Very likely because of his lean, muscular physique, Tina immediately thought of the waste management department, the hauling and lifting required in trash disposal.

No wonder he could eat like a racehorse and show not an inch of excess flesh, she mused. If, indeed, he was employed in the area of waste management.

Tina opened her mouth to ask point-blank, but Eric beat her into speech.

"More coffee?"

"Er...no, thank you." Tina shifted mental gears. "I'm stuffed to the gills."

"You ate the flounder's gills?" Eric opened his eyes wide in feigned horror.

"No, you idiot," Tina said, laughing. "The broiled flounder I ordered came sans gills."

"I didn't notice." He grinned at her. "But I am relieved to hear it."

"Of course you didn't notice," she gibed. "You were too busy inhaling two dozen steamed clams, a one-pound lobster tail, a baked potato, literally swimming in butter and sour cream, and a Caesar salad that looked large enough to feed a family of four."

"Only if they were on a strict diet," Eric protested in an injured tone.

Tina was helpless against the offended expression he pulled, and the laughter teasing her quivering lips. The question of his work went right out of her head. She didn't notice its departure, because she was too caught up in the sheer joy she experienced just being with him.

When Eric flashed his wicked grin, Tina's amusement escaped. They exited the restaurant laughing together, her cares forgotten, for tonight, at least.

That week alternately sped up or crawled by for Tina. When she was with Eric in the evening, the hours flew, seemingly contracting into mere moments. The opposite applied when she was away from him, minutes expanding into long hours.

Like greedy Midas, Tina and Eric hoarded their gold of hours; their favorite hiding place was Tina's bed.

And there, with all the verve and enthusiasm of intrepid adventurers, they eagerly explored the alluring terrain of each other's bodies, while probing the depths of their individual sensuality.

Tina had never before known such happiness, had never before basked in the unadulterated joy of just being alive.

Questions and doubts no longer picked with nervous little fingers at the fabric of her mind. Tina unhesitatingly admitted that she loved Eric with every particle of her being.

That is, she admitted it to *herself;* she had not murmured one word of love to him. Not because she was afraid to broach the subject; she wasn't. She firmly believed that he was as much in love with her as she was with him. His actions, his attitude, the glow in his crystal blue eyes when he looked at her, all spoke in silent eloquence of his love for her. No, she was not in the least afraid to speak the words.

Tina was simply waiting for Eric to speak them first.

The jury was no longer out; the verdict was in and emblazoned on his mind like the legendary words carved inside crudely rendered hearts on countless tree trunks.

Eric Wolfe loved Christina Kranas.

While he sat perched on the edge of the chair at the window, watching the house across the street, Eric came to the acceptance of his love for Tina. It was

Friday afternoon, one week to the day after his initial approach of her.

Was it really possible to fall in love in a week? Eric mused, stifling a yawn triggered by utter boredom. Must be, he reasoned, shifting to ease the numbness in his posterior. He was living proof of the possibility.

You ain't quite right, Wolfe, Eric chided himself, stretching his long legs out in front of him. Only a slightly bent cop would be dumb enough to fall for a suspect.

But was Tina still a suspect? Did he believe . . .

No. The denial leapt into Eric's head before the question of her association with the drug dealers was fully formed. Eric wasn't sure exactly when he had reached the conclusion that Tina was innocent of any involvement in the illegal operation, but the precise date and time didn't matter.

He'd had a gut feeling about the veracity of the tip from his informant, and he now had the same gut feeling about Tina's innocence.

Bottom line was, Eric trusted Tina, as well as loved her. He knew, unequivocally, that should the necessity arise he could trust her with his life.

Eric did not expect such a necessity to ever arise. He was capable of taking care of himself. And yet the rock-solid belief he now held that Tina would be there if he should need her assistance, regardless of the possible danger, was both comforting and exciting, for one thrilling reason.

Tina loved him.

Though she had not once mentioned the word *love* to him, Eric was as certain that Tina loved him as he was that the sun would continue to rise in the east.

He knew. How could he not know? Eric mused, sketching an image of Tina inside his mind, while keeping a sharp-eyed watch on the quiet street outside.

Tina had betrayed herself, her love, to him in a hundred ways, some barely noticeable, others so obvious they were soul-shattering . . . shattering *his* soul.

Tina had given the gift of herself, all of herself, to him in sweet and hot surrender. Eric treasured her gift, and her, and had offered the gift of himself in return.

Tina was his; he was hers. Her softness buffered his hardness. Her gentleness tempered his cynicism. The radiance in her lightened the darkness in him.

And the hardness, cynicism and darkness had been there, a living part of him, for a long time.

Eric shuddered, recalling the bitter hatred that had seared his mind, coloring his perception, on the day the minister intoned the service of burial over his father's casket.

He had lived for years with the bitterness and hatred eating away at him like an acid toxin.

Tina's very softness, her loving and laughter were Eric's antidote, the remedy that made him feel whole again. And, from his new perspective, he saw himself as the protector of her softness, the rock-solid strength between Tina and the harmful, seamy side of the world.

They were made for each other.

Someday soon, hopefully very soon, Eric would feel free to speak the four words he would not allow himself to say aloud until this surveillance was over, and she knew exactly who he was, what he was. Until then, he held them close, in his mind, in his heart, keeping them pure, for her alone.

I love you, Tina.

Some cop he was. The derisive thought brought a whimsical smile to Eric's compressed lips. He had spent more time loving Tina this week than watching the neighbors for continuing illegal developments.

Oh, well, it was his own time that he was squandering, he reminded himself.

Thing was, Eric didn't consider the time squandered. He regarded it as time well spent on every hope and dream he had once held for the future.

There would undoubtedly be many more undercover stakeouts down the road for him, Eric knew. But there was only one Tina.

She came first. As Maddy had always been to Eric's father, Tina was his top priority.

Love sure did strange things to folks.

The thought amused Eric, and he was still grinning some time later when the phone rang.

Since Eric had only given the number to two other people besides Cameron, the caller had to be either his boss or his love. Anticipation caused a tingle in the fingers that reached for the receiver.

"Eric?" The upbeat sound of Tina's voice did a tap dance on his nervous system.

"You were expecting Kevin Costner?" Eric asked in a teasing drawl.

"What would I want with him, when I can have you?" Tina asked in a solemn, serious tone that stole his breath, liquefied his insides and made mush of his brain.

"Eric?" she prodded uncertainly when he didn't respond for a couple of long seconds. "Did I say the wrong thing?"

"No, love," he assured her, pulling his wits together. "You said exactly the right thing."

"I meant it."

"I know." Eric grabbed for a steadying breath. "The knowing's driving me nuts."

"What do you mean?" Tina sounded confused, and a little worried. "I mean, why is it driving you nuts?"

"Because you're there, and I'm here," Eric said. "I'm missing you like hell."

"I'm missing you, too." Tina's voice was throaty, soft, and misty sounding.

It went to Eric's head, and his heart, and other vulnerable parts of his anatomy. Telling himself to lighten up before he started babbling his feelings to her like a love-struck teenager, he cleared his throat and said the first crazy thing that jumped into his head.

"You wanna have phone sex?"

Tina's laughter sang along the wire to him, tickling his ear, and his fancy. "Heavens, no!" she exclaimed. "Maybe I'm just old-fashioned, but I prefer the genuine article."

"Yeah, so do I," he purred. "When?"

"You're insatiable," she accused, still laughing.

"Yeah," he growled. "When?"

"Later tonight," she promised, in a thrill-inducing whisper. "But first..." She hesitated; he jumped in.

"First?"

"I was wondering if you felt like going out for a while this evening."

Things clicked in Eric's mind, bits of information came together. It was Friday, the night Tina usually spent in the company of her friends.

"The tavern?" he asked, knowing the answer.

"Yes," Tina answered, as expected. "Ted called me a little while ago to ask if I needed a lift tonight." She gave a half laugh. "To tell the truth, until he called, I'd completely forgotten about meeting the gang tonight."

Her admission pleased Eric very much. Enough to make him feel willing to share a portion of their time together with her friends.

"Okay. What time?"

There was a brief but telling silence. Eric smiled with tender understanding. Tina had expected him to balk at her suggestion of an outing.

"You want to go?" Tina's voice conveyed her surprise.

Eric smiled. "Sure. Why not?"

"Well, I thought that—" Tina paused, as if gathering her thoughts "—I thought you might prefer to stay in."

"A change of scenery couldn't hurt," Eric said in a slow drawl. "We haven't been out of the house together since Monday evening." He chuckled softly. "Hell, we've hardly been out of the bedroom since Monday evening."

"I wasn't bored." Tina's voice was so low he could barely hear it, and yet the message came through loud and clear. "Were you?"

"You know better than that." Eric's voice was also low, velvety with intimacy. "I loved every minute of it." Then he turned the tables on her. "Didn't you?"

"Yes," Tina whispered. "That's why I thought..." Her voice faded away.

"You thought correctly," Eric said, filling in the void. "But we must eat, too, keep up our strength." He paused for a reaction from her. When there was none, he continued. "I was assuming we were going to have dinner at the tavern."

"We were."

"Okay, then, we'll go," he said. "We can always come home early, you know."

"Yes, I do know," she agreed, in a purring tone that set his imagination on fire. "Suppose I swing by and pick you up after work? Say about six-thirty?"

"Or I could take the bike and meet you there," he suggested, to save her the run out of her way.

"But then we couldn't go home together," she pointed out in a senses-stirring purr.

"True," Eric said, not only taking her point, but running with it. "I'll be ready and waiting."

Agreeing to Tina's suggestion was the easy part for Eric. Getting through the rest of the afternoon was the hard part. Not a damn thing was happening in or around the house across the street. But that no longer bothered or surprised him.

Eric's familiar and trusted gut feeling had come back into play, and he had arrived at the conclusion that nothing was going to happen—not before the weekend. Instinct, or intuition, or something, had convinced him that whatever was going down over there was going down on Sundays.

Still, Eric watched, bored but diligent, until it was time to get himself ready for Tina.

All in all, the evening turned out to be rather enjoyable for Eric. Disarmed, so to speak, by the information his brother had provided about the members of the group, Eric felt more relaxed in their company, less constrained in joining in with the banter and harmless fun.

And he did have fun, more than he had allowed himself to indulge in for some length of time. He laughed at their jokes, even the lame ones, and even loosened up enough to offer a few dry witticisms of his own.

Yet, true to form, even as he relaxed and enjoyed, Eric dissected the reasons he had lowered his guard. First and foremost of these, of course, was the very fact of Cameron's verbal report that from all he could gather, every member of the group was clean, in the legal sense.

The second reason was the confirmation of Eric's initial perception of the members of the bunch being average, normal, genuinely nice people.

The third reason, and by far the most important to Eric, was the reflection on Tina's character by her very association with them. A reflection of character that coincided with his own independently drawn conclusions.

Birds of a feather, and all that.

So the evening proved a double success. Eric enjoyed himself, and Tina was happy. He was content to bask in the overflow of her happiness. She displayed it in the most exciting ways—after they had returned to her house, and to her bedroom.

It began snowing in fits and starts of flurries early Sunday morning. By midday the fitful snowfall was dusting lawns, shrubs and tree branches, but was still melting on the sidewalks and streets.

"Isn't it pretty?" Tina said in delight. "I have always loved the first snowfall of the season."

"It won't last," Eric predicted, softening his observation with a smile. "Too early."

"I suppose," she murmured. "Thanksgiving is still over a week and a half away."

"Yeah," he murmured, turning his gaze from the window to the paper he held in his hand. "Besides, the bad-driving weather will come soon."

Tina shuddered. "That's the minus side of snow, driving in it. I get nervous just— Oh, hell!" she muttered.

Eric raised his glance from the sports page to frown at her. "What's the matter?"

"It's my ex-husband." She grimaced and indicated the street with a sharp movement of her head. "I hope he's not thinking of stopping in here—" Tina broke off on a groan, then said in disgust, "Oh, nuts, here he comes."

"So I see." Eric was already on his feet, the paper still clutched in one hand. His brain shifted into high gear as his eyes narrowed on the confident-looking man just then stepping onto the front stoop, beneath the protective overhang.

Well, surprise, surprise, Eric thought wryly. It must be Sunday... day of deliverance.

The doorbell rang.

Tina groaned again.

"Are you afraid of him?" Eric sliced a hard look at her. "Because if you are, there's no reason for you to be, not as long as I'm here."

"I'm not." Tina shook her head and stood up as the bell rang once more. "I'm tired of telling him I'm not interested—not in him, or his friends." She jerked her head, indicating the house across the street. "I want him to leave me alone."

"Would you like me to convey that message to him from you?" Eric asked in a soft, deadly-sounding voice.

Tina looked startled for an instant. Then she laughed, a little shakily. "Good heavens, Eric, lighten up. You look positively lethal." She started for the door, tossing over her shoulder, "You don't want me to be afraid of you, do you?" she said teasingly, turning away to open the door.

Good advice, that, so back off, Wolfe, Eric told himself. It was going to be hard enough telling her about himself when the time came. He certainly didn't want her afraid of him, not now, not ever.

Taut but controlled, Eric listened to the exchange between Tina and Glen Reber filtering to him from the doorway.

"No, Glen," she was saying adamantly. "I am not going to invite you in."

"But why not?" he persisted angrily. "It's snowing and it's cold out here."

"Go visit your friends across the street," she said with obvious impatience. "Their house is as warm as mine."

"This used to be my house, too."

"Used to be is as dead as the bad relationship we once shared," Tina retorted. "I told you before that I don't want you coming around anymore, Glen. I meant it. If you do, I won't answer the door."

"You always were a cold bitch," he snarled.

He'd deck the bastard.

Fury impelled Eric into motion. He was halfway to the door when Tina shut it in Glen's face. Fortunately for Eric, she stood staring at the solid panels for a few moments, long enough for him to return to his position near the window and conceal his dangerous intent behind an expressionless mask of calm.

You'll get yours, creep. Someday. Soon. And the pleasure will be all mine.

Through eyes glittering with the promise of retribution, Eric watched Glen storm away from the door, down the glistening walk, and then to the house across the street.

"He's gone."

"I know." Consciously relaxing his battle-tightened muscles, Eric consigned Glen Reber to a day of reckoning and turned from the window to smile at her. "If he bothers you again, let me know," he said, careful to keep his voice cool and steady, his smile easy.

"I don't think he will." She sighed tiredly. "At least I hope this time I got through to him."

"And if you didn't, I'll take care of it," he assured her, feeling the weight of her sigh.

"No!" Tina said sharply, her face paling. "I don't want you involved with him."

Eric frowned, feeling an instant's doubt about her own involvement with Reber. Then he immediately dismissed it. He wasn't wrong, but something was.

"Why?" he demanded.

"Because I don't want you hurt!" Tina exclaimed.

Eric smiled.

"Oh, men and their damn macho image!" Tina glared at him. "Eric, you don't understand."

"So enlighten me."

"Glen is dangerous." Her eyes lost their sparkle, growing dark and bleak. "I... I learned after the divorce that Glen had been arrested, several times. Once for nearly killing a man with a knife." Beginning to tremble, she sank onto the edge of the sofa. "I couldn't bear it if you—" Her voice broke, and she stared at him in abject fear.

Eric crossed to her in three long strides. Grasping her shoulders, he drew her up and into his arms. "Tina, don't look like that," he murmured, soothing her with a gentle stroke of his hand down her back. "Honey... honey, nothing's going to happen to me." He grinned. "I'm tough."

"But, Glen's—" She broke off once more, shuddering.

"A two-bit hood," Eric said with casual unconcern. Then he frowned. "And I'm damned if I can figure out how a woman like you ever got tangled up with a lowlife like him."

"I was a fool." Tina's pale cheeks flared pink. "A young, naive fool." She lowered her eyes in embarrassment. "And Glen can put on quite a performance. He can turn on the charm until it practically oozes out of his pores. He set a romantic scene, and cast himself as Prince Charming. I bought the play from opening night. He swept me off my feet, and kept my head spinning right up to the altar." She expelled a short, harsh laugh. "I learned the meaning of duplicity on my wedding night."

"Dare I ask how?"

"No." Tina shook her head. "I don't want to think about it, let alone talk about it. It's over. Done. And I'm no longer a naive young fool."

"No, you aren't," Eric murmured, slowing lowering his head. "You are a beautiful, exciting temptress."

She started to laugh at his description of her, but her laughter got lost inside his mouth.

It wasn't far from the kiss to the floor.

Holding her as if she were made of the most delicate china, Eric gently drew her down with him to the carpet; it made a viable subsitute bed.

Following the lead of an emotional need he had never before experienced, Eric did not so much make love to Tina as give physical expression to how much he cherished her.

Nevertheless, the results were the same.

Murmuring to her, caressing her, stroking her silky skin with feather-light brushes of his hands and lips and tongue, he kindled a spark that quickly burst into flames that swiftly went racing out of control.

"Eric."

His name on her lips, softly pleading, enticing, set Eric's pulses beating against his eardrums. The glide of her fingertips down the length of his spine drew a shuddering breath from his constricted chest.

Eric fought against the tide of desire threatening to overtake them both. It was a losing battle.

Passion escalated. Hands skimmed. Mouths fused. Tongues dueled. Bodies joined.

Hold on. Hold on.

Eric repeated the words to him himself in a desperate bid to draw every drop of sweetness from the moment. Loving Tina, giving of himself, as he had never loved or given to any other woman, he expanded the moment to the outer limits of endurance.

Then the moment exploded.

Eric felt shattered. Undone. Wonderful.

The descent from the heights was slow. When his breathing leveled and his heart felt as if it would stay inside his chest, instead of hammering its way out, Eric stretched out on the floor beside Tina, drew her close to his quivering body and was asleep within seconds.

The chill in the air woke Eric. He felt stiff, and cramped, but most of all he felt cold. The room was dark except for the pale glow from the picture window. Beyond the pane, he could see large, lacy snowflakes swirling in the wind.

Shivering, Eric swept his hand along the carpet until he found his shirt. Sitting up, he spread the shirt over Tina. Then, groaning silently at the stiffness of his muscles, he rolled away from her and stumbled to his feet.

Standing stark naked in the middle of the room, stretching and flexing to work the kinks from his body, Eric stared through the window at the snow. He was about to turn away, intending to scoop up Tina and carry her into the shower, when the flare of headlights, reflecting brightly off the snow, snagged his attention and kept him still. Behind the snow-sparkled pool of light crept a full-size, closed van.

Suddenly alert and taut with expectancy, Eric watched the van come to a halt, then slowly turn into the driveway of the house down the street.

"Damned fool."

Cursing himself aloud for surrendering to his clamoring senses on this night of all nights, Eric turned this way, then that way, searching the darkened floor for his pants, unaware that he was firing off a string of colorful curses of self-condemnation.

"Eric, what's wrong?" Tina's voice was blurry with sleep and confusion.

"I've got to hurry," he muttered, zipping his pants as he shoved a bare foot into a shoe.

"But...why?"

"Because I want to get closer to watch," he answered distractedly, searching out his other shoe.

"Closer?" Hugging the shirt to her, Tina scrambled up off the floor. "Watch for what?"

"The delivery of drugs," Eric said without thinking. "In that house of your ex's friends, across the street."

"Drug delivery?" Tina cried. "You can't be serious!"

"I'm dead serious." Eric was nearly growling now, furious at himself and the elusive shoe. And he didn't think to guard his tongue. "I witnessed a delivery there last week."

"I can't believe it." Tina shivered, and pulled the shirt tightly, protectively around her shaking body.

"Ah..." Eric purred, spying the shoe. He pushed his foot into it, then headed for the dining room and the small closet where Tina had hung his coat earlier.

"Where are you going?"

Eric wasn't startled by her sudden appearance; quiet as she had been, he'd heard every move she made. He shrugged into his jacket as he turned to her.

"I told you. I want a closer look." Stepping around her, he started for the kitchen, which was dimly lit by the night-light on the stove. "I'll go out the back."

"Eric!" Tina called, running after him and clutching at his arm. "If there is some sort of drug dealing going on over there, you could be in terrible danger."

"I must go, Tina," he said impatiently, pulling his arm back to loosen her grasp; she hung on tight.

"Why?" she shouted, giving a yank on his arm hard enough to turn him halfway around. "Why you?"

"Who, then?" Eric snapped, out of patience.

"The police!" she shouted, wincing as he jerked his arm free of her clutching fingers.

"I *am* the police."

Ten

I am the police.

Eric's flatly voiced statement echoing in her head, Tina stood, still as a post, staring at the back door in wide-eyed disbelief.

"A cop," she murmured dully. "Eric's a cop."

Questions tumbled into her mind.

How had Eric known there would be a delivery of drugs tonight to the house across the street? How long had he known? Had he moved into the neighborhood to keep that house under surveillance? Why hadn't he told her? Had he had her under surveillance, real close surveillance, as well?

Could Eric possibly have believed that she was involved with whatever was going on over there?

Tina could handle the barrage of questions; what she couldn't deal with were the obvious answers.

A queasy sensation invaded her stomach. A chill ran the length of her small form, a chill unrelated to the scant protection of the cotton shirt draping her otherwise nude body from shoulders to midthigh.

Eric's shirt. And Eric was a cop.

So, what did that make her?

A dupe . . . again.

"Oh, God." Tina's stomach lurched, and, flinging a hand up to clap it over her mouth, she whirled and made a headlong dash for the bathroom.

Eric watched the red taillights blink, and then the van turned right at the end of the street. He pushed up his jacket sleeve and glanced at his watch. The hands stood at 8:16. His lips twisted into a wry smile.

Later than last week . . . but still in the ballpark, he mused, recalling the previous Sunday's delivery. But then it had been furniture. Tonight it had been small white cartons marked Fine Crystal in large black letters.

Crystal. Right.

Eric snorted. And then he sneezed.

Hell, he was freezing. And no wonder, he thought, sliding his hands into the jacket's slash side pockets. He'd run out of Tina's little more than half-dressed.

Tina!

"Oh, sh—" Eric's voice was carried off by the wind as he turned away from his position at a corner of the house directly across the street from the one under surveillance.

Retracing his tracks along the unpaved alley behind the homes lining the street, Eric approached Tina's back door with a mounting sense of apprehension. His unease owed everything to his sudden recollection of having blurted out not only his suspicions about the drug dealing, but also his true occupation.

"Damn," Eric cursed, grasping the doorknob. He had one whole hell of a lot of explaining to do. He only hoped Tina would be willing to listen.

No, his first hope was that she had not thought to relock the door. Holding his breath, he twisted the knob and gave a gentle push. The door swung open.

"Thank you, Jesus," Eric whispered fervently. "Now, I may not deserve it, but if you'll only hang in there with me a mite longer, I'd surely appreciate it, Sir."

Moving as silently as smoke, Eric stepped into the kitchen and quietly shut the door. He saw her even before he reached the archway into the dining room. Apparently she had showered, for her hair was a dark and damp mass of loose waves cascading around her shoulders. She was dressed in faded jeans and an oversize green-and-white Eagles sweatshirt.

Eric sighed; she had looked so damn sexy in nothing but his shirt. He stared at her longingly a moment, then strode through the dining room.

"Tina."

Tina started at the sudden, unexpected sound of her name, but caught back the scream that filled her throat.

Eric!

She had deliberately curled up on the chair by the window so that she couldn't possibly miss his approach to the front door—if he had the gall to return. And here he was, standing bold as sin in her living room!

Scrambling out of the chair, Tina drew herself up to her full five-foot-two-and-three-quarter-inch height, planted her hands on her hips and glared him straight in the eyes.

"How did you get in here?" she demanded. "Do you have a damned master key or something?"

"Of course not." Eric took a step closer. She narrowed her eyes. He stepped back. "You forgot to relock the door after I went out."

"Well, you can just go right back out again," she said in an emotionally strained voice. "And believe me, I won't forget to lock the door after you."

"Tina, listen . . ." he began in a soothing tone.

"I don't want to listen to anything you have to say," Tina cut him off. "I just want you to go." A curl of disdain lifted the corner of her lip. "Officer Wolfe."

"I couldn't tell you." Eric raked a hand through his snow-dampened tawny hair. "You have to understand—"

Tina again ruthlessly interrupted him. "Oh, I understand. Boy, do I understand. I worked it all out while I was waiting for you to show your face again . . . if you had the nerve."

"Nerve has nothing to do with it," Eric said, trying another tentative step.

"Stay right where you are!" Tina's barely controlled voice cracked like a whip.

Eric came to a halt . . . two steps closer to her.

It was much too close for Tina's peace of mind. She wanted to punch him out, tear into him with her fingernails, do severe bodily damage to him. She wanted to score his skin, make him hurt on the surface as much as she was hurting inside.

"Tina, please," he said with edgy patience. "If you'd just let me explain, talk to you."

"Now he wants to talk to me, explain," she said to the air around her. "He thinks I'm stupid. . . . Ha! What am I saying? I *am* stupid!"

"Tina!"

"You lied to me!"

"I didn't."

"Oh, right." She laughed derisively. "You just conveniently omitted telling me what department you worked in for the city. Lord only knows what else you omitted telling me. Things like suspecting me of being involved with drug dealing...or whatever is going on across the street...simply because I was once married to Glen."

"But only at first," he said defensively.

"Only at first," she repeated, feeling sicker with each passing second.

Eric was beginning to look harried, and tired. "Can't we sit down and talk this out?"

"No." Tina shook her head, and swallowed the acrid taste of loss. "No, Eric. I don't want to talk to you. I can't bear the thought of talking with a man who will go to any lengths, even to making love to me, to use me."

"I did not." Eric's voice was hard; his eyes were harder, glittering like frozen chunks of morning sky.

Tina knew she had to end this, get him out of her house. Because she was weakening, beginning to long to believe him, she was vulnerable.

"Get out of here, Eric," she said, in a voice made cold by the fear of her love for him.

"All right." He sighed, and it was then that she noticed he was shivering. "I'll go."

"Don't forget your shirt." Tina moved her hand to indicate the garment draped over an arm of the sofa.

Eric grabbed his shirt and strode to the door. Then he turned to look at her. "But I'll be back, Tina, after you've had a chance to cool down."

"That'll be never," Tina said, wishing he would just go, before the tears stinging her eyes betrayed her by spilling over onto her cheeks. "Twice burned, and all that."

He just stood there, staring at her, staring, as if imprinting every one of her features on his mind. Then, finally, he turned, pulled open the door and left.

And not an instant too soon. Tina collapsed onto the carpet, wrenching sobs racking her trembling body before the door clicked shut.

Eric sneezed. Then he coughed. Then he swore. He had developed a head cold. Happens when a man stands in the snow only partially dressed, he thought, sneezing again.

Some two inches of snow had accumulated on the ground by late Sunday night. It had turned to mush, then melted entirely by sundown Monday...along about the time Eric began sneezing in earnest.

By Tuesday night, he felt lousy...but not only from the effects of the viral infection. Tina had adamantly refused to talk to him . . . twice.

Eric had called her early Monday morning... between sneezes. In a tone of voice at least twenty degrees colder than the outside temperature, Tina had told him, in a scathing tone, to drop dead.

By the next morning, Eric had felt that he just might comply, but, undaunted, he'd dialed her number again.

She'd hung up on him.

Deciding that perhaps Tina needed a little more cooling-off time, Eric resisted the gnawing desire to call her on Wednesday. He called his boss instead.

His trusted gut feeling had joined forces with his standby hunch, and both were telling him the big shipment was due...probably this coming Sunday. Eric figured it was time to apprise his superior of the situation.

"I had a sneaky suspicion you were up to something," Lieutenant Dan Phillips drawled after Eric finished telling his story. "You, on vacation. Ha."

"You wound me." Eric grinned, then sneezed.

"Yeah, well, get yourself and your wound downtown," Dan retorted. "We've got an operation to set up."

By Friday, everything was in place. Eric was feeling slightly better...at least as far as his head cold was concerned. But he was missing Tina more than he would have believed himself capable of ever missing any one individual.

Wanting Tina, wanting just to be with her, was driving him crazy. Eric consoled himself with a promise to confront her as soon as this drug business was over, and convince her of his love for her, on his knees, if necessary.

He fervently hoped that wouldn't be necessary.

Tina had a miserable week.

Business at the shop was brisk. She was making

money. But she couldn't work up any enthusiasm about either the business or the profits.

She missed Eric so badly she felt like screaming. . . primarily at him for not being the man he had led her to believe he was. . .damn his lying soul.

By closing time on Friday, Tina was exhausted. It was hard work acting as if she didn't have a care in the world, to stave off speculation and questions from her assistant, and being pleasant and helpful to her customers.

Using the old-standby excuse of a headache, Tina did not join her friends at the tavern on Friday evening. By Saturday evening, the excuse had become a reality.

Tina swallowed two aspirins and crawled into bed as soon as she got home from work.

She didn't sleep; she cried.

By morning the headache and the tears were gone. Tina had found something more important to replace them. It was Sunday. She knew from what Eric had let slip that he suspected the drug deliveries were made on Sundays.

Tina didn't have time for a headache or tears; she was too busy worrying herself frantic about Eric.

By sundown, Tina was pacing the house like a crazed lioness forcibly separated from her cubs.

It was after six-thirty when she saw Glen's distinctive Lincoln moving slowly down the street. She held her breath, then let it out on a relieved sigh when, instead of heading straight for her door after parking his car in front of her place, as he had the two previous Sundays, he crossed the street and went directly to his friends' house.

Afraid to move away from the window, and too keyed up to sit, Tina stood back a ways from the glass pane, waiting, and watching, and wondering if Eric was watching, too.

It was nearing nine-thirty when Tina saw the vehicle lumbering down the street. Without pausing to consider or even think, she flew to the phone and dialed Eric's number. The minute she heard his voice, she blurted out the information.

"Eric, there's a motor home coming down the street!"

"I see it." He voice was terse, clipped. "Stay inside, Tina. And that's an official order."

"Be careful, Eric. I—" Tina broke off; Eric had disconnected. "I love you," she whispered too low for him to hear. Then, replacing the receiver, she ran back to the window.

Eric was tense with anticipation, poised for the coming action. Yet inside, a glimmer of hope sent tendrils of warmth curling around his heart.

Tina had cared enough to warn him.

It wasn't as good as a declaration of love, but it was something to hang on to.

His full attention now on the business at hand, Eric watched, a satisfied smile quirking his lips, as Glen Reber and Bob Freeman exited the house and strode to the RV. As the two men drew close to the vehicle, the door opened and another man handed out two large suitcases.

Eric activated his two-way radio.

"Company's here." he said tersely. "I'm going to a party. Wanna come?"

Turning from the window, Eric made his way unerringly through the dark room to the door.

An RV, of all things, he thought, shaking his head as he descended the outside stairs three at a time. Before he had traversed the short distance from the stairs to the end of the driveway, the street was swarming with cops, every one of them converging on the RV and the men lugging the cases toward the house.

How Glen Reber managed to slip through the human strands of that closing net, Eric would never figure out, but slip through it he did.

Eric had crossed the sidewalk, blending into the darkness next to a curbside tree, when he spotted Reber, hugging the inky darkness around the home next to the target house, inching his way down the street to his car.

Leaping into the road, Eric took off at a run after the retreating man. By the time he arrived in the general area where he knew his quarry should be, Reber had vanished.

Taking slow, quiet, measured breaths, Eric began a game of hide-and-seek.

Eric lost. His quarry found him first. He was four houses down from the action, across the street from Reber's car, and Tina's house, when he felt the unmistakable feeling of a knife point pressed against the side of his neck, directly above his jugular vein.

"No heroics, tall man," Reber warned in a grating whisper close to Eric's ear. "If you want to keep the blood flowing inside that vein, you'll move slow and careful toward that car over there." He backed up the threat with an added bit of pressure from the knife.

Eric's parents had not raised any fools. Biding his time, watching and waiting for the right moment, he began moving, slowly, carefully, toward the big Lincoln.

With his attention divided between his captive and his car, Reber never gave so much as a glance to his ex-wife's house. He should have. He didn't see her.

But Eric did. And his blood ran ice-cold.

Jesus, Tina, stop!

The cry rang inside Eric's head as he watched her emerge from the shadows beneath the overhang. Her hands gripping the handle of the large black iron frying pan she was holding high over her head, Tina came running down the walkway toward them.

Right or wrong, his moment was upon him. Eric seized it. He moved with blurring swiftness. Ignoring the pinprick of the knife point puncturing his skin, he raised his arm and his knee as he turned.

Three things happened simultaneously.

The hard outer edge of his hand slashed down into the curve of Reber's neck.

His knee smashed into the man's groin.

And the frying pan landed with a thunk on Glen's head.

Reber grunted, then dropped to the street like a stone.

"Oh my god!" Tina cried. "Is he dead?"

Hunching down, Eric pressed his fingers to the side of Reber's throat. "Nah," he said, springing upright. "But he'll hurt like hell when he comes to."

"Eric...I..." She broke off, staring at him through eyes widened from reaction. "You're bleeding!"

Raising his hand, Eric touched his fingers to the wet trickle seeping from the wound. "It's nothing."

"It—it's over?" Her voice quavered, her body shook, the pan hanging at her side from her limp hand swayed.

"It's over." Eric was fully aware of the commotion around the house up the street, the raised voices calling back and forth, the red-and-blue lights flashing atop the police cars filling the roadway. And yet he saw only Tina, and he saw red, a surge of anger born of fear.

He opened his mouth to give her a blistering lecture, dress her down one side and up the other for endangering herself by disobeying his orders to remain inside.

The words caught in his throat, as through his mind flashed the memory of his thoughts the previous week, his belief that he could trust Tina with his life if necessary.

She had run to his defense.

But she had put herself in jeopardy, Eric reminded himself. She could have been seriously injured...or worse. The feeling inside him swirled again, now more fear than anger. He had to make her understand the magnitude of the risk she'd taken. His lips parted once more.

"I love you, Tina."

She gasped and stared at him, dumbfounded, and then the pan hit the sidewalk with a clang and she turned and ran back into the house.

It was late when Eric was at last free to leave the police station. A co-worker dropped him off at his center-city apartment.

Forty minutes later, showered, shaved and dressed in brown slacks, a white turtleneck and a tweed jacket, Eric emerged from the underground parking garage driving his late-model midsize car.

Now that the drug-shipment business was over, he had a real job of work to do...that of convincing a certain small, beautiful, risk-taking, breathtaking blonde that they were made for each other.

Eric prayed she would listen.

Tina sat curled up in the chair by the window. Hers was the only house on the block with lights spilling into the one o'clock a.m. darkness.

Her features were composed. Her hands lay at rest in the velvet softness of the green ankle-length robe covering her lap. Her eyes stared into the night. Watching. Waiting. Listening for the low roar of the monster machine.

A tiny frown line appeared between her pale eyebrows when, instead of the bike, a silver-gray car came down the street and made the turn into her driveway.

Tina's pulse leapt with combined anticipation and panic on sight of the tall form that stepped from the car and moved with purposeful strides to her front door. She sprang from the chair, the full skirt of the robe swirling around her legs as she took off at a run. She was at the door before the sound of the first ring of the bell faded on the air.

"May I come in?" Eric's voice was tense, strained; his sharply defined features were drawn to a fine edge.

Tina couldn't speak, for the emotion clogging her throat. Nodding in answer, she slowly backed away, all the way into the middle of the living room. Mute, she stared at him, absently noting how very handsome he looked.

His eyes, clear as a crisp, blue autumn sky, boring into hers, Eric stalked her to a standstill at the arm of the sofa.

"Are you ready to listen now?" His voice, low and taut with urgency, tingled from her nape to the base of her spine.

"Is that your car?" Tina moved her head a fraction, indicating the driveway.

"Yes." Eric frowned. "What does that have to do with anything? I asked if you were willing, now, to listen to my explanation?"

"No."

He went absolutely still. His face paled. A fine tremor shook his strong fingers. "No?"

Still unable to form words, Tina slowly moved her head back and forth in denial.

"Tina." Eric's voice was a whispered cry of agony torn from his throat.

Tina couldn't bear the sound of it. She took a hesitant step toward him.

He extended a hand, as if in supplication.

"I love you, Eric."

He froze. Then, a light bursting like blue fireworks in his eyes, he strode to her and pulled her into his arms.

"Tina... Tina, you had me so damned scared," he groaned, kissing her hair, her temple, her eyes, her cheeks. "If you ever endanger yourself like that again..."

"I'm sorry," Tina murmured, smoothing her hands over his hair, the high bones of his cheeks, his hard jaw. "But I was afraid, terrified Glen would hurt you."

"God, I love you." His mouth brushed hers. "Can you forgive me for not telling you who and what I am?"

"I have," she whispered, raising her mouth to his.

"Love me." It was not a question, but a plea.

"I do." Tina brushed his lips with her own. "Oh, Eric, I love you more than my own life."

"Then show me." Sweeping her up, close to the revealing thump of his heart in his chest, Eric strode for her bedroom.

She did.

* * * * *

MAN of the Month 1994

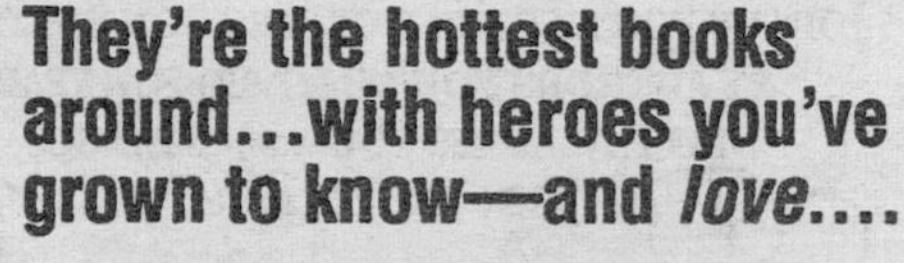

They're the hottest books around...with heroes you've grown to know—and *love*....

Created by top authors—the ones *you* say are your favorites....

Don't miss a single one of these handsome hunks—

In July
Wolfe Watching
by **Joan Hohl**

In August
Fusion
by **Cait London**

In September
Family Feud
by **Barbara Boswell**

In October
Temptation Texas Style!
by **Annette Broadrick**

In November
The Accidental Bridegroom
by **Ann Major**

In December
An Obsolete Man
by **Lass Small**

Man of the Month...only from Silhouette Desire

MOM94JD